Crime In Mind

Patsy Collins

Contents

1. Surprised To Death

One sunny afternoon, Detectives Susanna Murphy and Brad Reed were returning from an event where he'd been presented with a bravery award.

"I still think it should have been given to us both," he said. "I only knew which way to go because you told me, and I only got there first because I have longer legs."

Susanna pulled over and stopped the police car. "Rubbish. You were the one who got shot at and saved that kid."

"I suppose. Thanks for making me look like a hero anyway. Ah, just realised we're at the LeGrand mansion. You've stopped to take another peek at how the other half live, not just to bolster my ego."

"Actually, I've stopped because the gates which are always chained and locked are currently wide open. Any chance you can notice something suspicious and give us an excuse to go in for a look round?"

"Sorry, everything seems fine."

Susanna sighed dramatically. "You're the worst partner ever!"

"Yeah, sorry. Oh, can you hear a siren?"

"No... Yes! Ambulance and I think it's coming this way."

She was right. An ambulance roared down the road and swung in through the open gates.

"We should follow in case we can help," Brad said.

"I take it back about you being a rubbish partner," Susanna said as she followed the ambulance.

She saw immaculate lawns in front of sweeping steps, leading up to a terrace in front of a magnificent building. To her disappointment the ambulance didn't stop outside, but disappeared round the side and down a lane. When it eventually stopped, Susanna parked a short distance away, so as not to block the ambulance's way out, should it need to leave in a hurry.

A cluster of people were gathered around someone lying on the ground. Susanna and Brad asked them to move back to allow the paramedic to work, and tried to find out what was going on. After a while the paramedic shook his head to indicate he'd been unable to save his patient. Everyone else sat quietly together.

The detectives studied the scene, where a short time ago a family picnic had been taking place. The sun shone onto flower studded grass and glinted off crystal glasses. There were bottles of champagne in a huge, ice filled bucket. Serving platters were heaped with slices of smoked salmon, chicken portions, tiny crustless sandwiches and colourful salads. For dessert there were chocolate eclairs, individual lemon meringue pies, and fresh fruit in every colour of the rainbow from raspberries and apricots to blueberries. Close at hand was a stack of plates. A little further away were the inviting blue waters of the lake, surrounded by trees.

"Perfect, isn't it?" Susanna said.

"Not entirely," her colleague Brad replied. "The presence of a defeated looking paramedic, the body of Virginia LeGrand, and the shocked expressions of the people who'd come to celebrate her ninety-fifth birthday do slightly spoil it."

"I didn't mean the party, but the situation," Susanna explained. "It's private land and that bridge we crossed is the only way in. That means the party guests are our only suspects. We should have this solved in no time."

"I admire your optimism, but I don't understand why you're so sure this is a murder."

"Instinct, I suppose. But don't you think it's odd that none of them seemed surprised to see us?" she asked.

"Not really," Brad said. "They were most likely in shock over the death."

"And that's another thing. There are six of them – you'd expect at least one of them to know some first aid, but nobody was trying to revive her."

"She was old and frail. They may have realised there was nothing to be done," Brad said. That's the way the two detectives liked to work – both presenting opposite points of view until one had convinced the other they were correct. Which of course meant they discussed the case until Brad realised Susanna was right yet again.

The paramedic joined them. "It was almost certainly her heart," he said. "That tallies with what the family said. Poor woman needn't have died – they knew enough to have prevented it!"

"Seems your instinct was right," Brad said.

Once the dead woman had been lifted into the ambulance and driven away, the detectives approached their suspects.

"Can you tell us who you all are and exactly what happened?" Brad asked.

"I'm Peter LeGrand, that's my sister Nancy." He gestured to a young woman and then introduced Samuel Brown, siblings Joe and Betty Davis, and Kimberley LeGrand.

"We're all cousins and Virginia LeGrand is our great aunt, although we called her Aunt Gin. And, as I'm sure you want to know, she was very rich and we all inherit equally."

"Whose idea was this picnic?"

"Peter started the ball rolling," Samuel said. "By suggesting we all come for a celebration."

"That's right." Peter hung his head. "At the time it seemed such a nice idea…"

"I can see this is difficult, but we do need to know exactly what happened."

"I stayed over with Aunt Gin last night, and everyone else arrived this morning, bringing the food, drink and so on."

"Aunt Gin wasn't the sort to eat off plastic, so I brought china plates and crystal glasses," said Kimberly.

"I brought the drinks," Nancy said. "And everyone else contributed the food."

"You set up the picnic, then what?" Susanna asked.

"I walked out with Aunt Gin," Peter said. "And everyone called 'surprise' as we came round the corner." He glared at his cousins. "Maybe not the best idea with her heart."

"You all knew about that?" Susanna asked.

"Yes," Peter admitted, "But that didn't stop Kimberly popping a champagne cork, or Betty sneezing."

"I didn't do it on purpose!" Betty insisted. "You know I get hay fever every spring."

"And all these sudden noises brought on her heart attack?" Brad asked.

"She keeled right over," Peter confirmed. "I sent Joe to the house to get her pills from the hall table, but she was dead by the time he got back."

Brad and Susanna moved aside to confer.

"We'll need to take statements," Brad said. "But that won't tell us whether it was Nancy with the champagne, Betty deliberately sneezing or Joe taking too long to fetch the pills which caused her death."

"You're right we must take statements, but they don't have to tell us what happened, as I already know."

"What exactly do you know?" Brad asked.

"The cousins all seem very close, don't they?"

"Very much so! Ah, so they were all in on it and did it by calling out 'surprise'?"

"No, but they'd probably all know about Betty's hay fever and that she'd be liable to sneeze."

"And that Nancy would bring champagne – that's why Kimberly brought the fancy glasses. Oh, wasn't she the one who popped the cork?"

"She was, but it wasn't her fault Ms LeGrand died."

"No. Those tablets would have saved her. So it was Joe! He took too long fetching them?"

"Nobody has suggested he was slow, but it's quite a long way back to the house and he had to find them."

"Shouldn't have taken long – Peter told him they were on the hall table."

"That's the same Peter who planned this party, knew how his cousins would react, and walked the old lady out, leaving behind the tablets he knew she was likely to need."

"You're right. Maybe we won't be able to prove it, but he is responsible."

"Of course we'll prove it, Brad!"

"Yes, I expect you will – and share the glory with me yet again. I've got one thing absolutely right though."

"Which is?" Susanna asked.

"We'll need to do a very thorough search for evidence in that mansion you're always craning your neck to get a glimpse of, every time we pass."

"I always said you're the best partner ever."

2. All In The Planning

Some people think I'm a doormat. The Cookes next door certainly did when it came to their planning application. They were wrong though, I'm not like that really. I just think it's best to stick to the rules and handle any disputes as quietly, and with as little fuss, as possible. Better yet, give it a chance to blow over or for someone else to sort it out without my needing to get involved. Might not sound much of a plan, but it often works.

Take the time the Cookes went away and their teenage kids had a really noisy party. I could have gone round and yelled at them to be quiet, but that wouldn't have been very friendly and the kids didn't really mean any harm. I just put up with the racket until midnight and then went in to work. Someone told me the police had arrived at three and made arrests, but there was no sign of trouble by the time I came home.

Calm negotiation can work too. My daughter once complained, "It isn't fair. Everyone else has them," when I said she couldn't have the ridiculously expensive trainers she wanted. I could have lied and said the shop had sold out, or snapped that life wasn't fair, but I gently reasoned with her.

"Do you really want to follow the herd and be just like everyone else?" I asked.

Actually that isn't such a great example as she said yes, so I had to get her a pair. You get the idea though and that was a long time ago. She's married and got her own baby on the way now.

When I discovered what my husband was really doing when he stayed late at the office I could have screamed an ultimatum, then slung him and all his stuff out onto the street. I didn't. OK, I still lost him, but I kept my dignity. I'm not so wet I could forgive and forget having my trust deliberately abused, so ensured my lawyer negotiated a good financial settlement. I like my new, smaller but mortgage free, home. For a while I didn't, but I do now.

The Cookes weren't exactly the best of neighbours. It took me a while to work that out. At first they seemed fine. Noisy, but fine. There were a lot of them, so often their cars were parked outside my house, sometimes partially over my driveway. Some people might have complained, but as long as I could get in and out, I tried not to let it worry me.

The houses are semi-detached halves of the same building. Before I bought my half, the surveyor informed me the roof would soon be in need of attention. I was pleased when the Cookes mentioned they were having theirs fixed and suggested it was all done at once to save costs. When the bill was considerably higher than the surveyor's estimate I was less happy. After discovering the firm who'd done the job were close friends of the Cookes, I was suspicious.

Had those friends taken advantage of them? I knew from experience that kind of thing can happen. It's tricky. You don't want to risk upsetting them and saying anything if there's a chance you're wrong. On the other hand, if you're right, then the people aren't friends at all and you're better off without them. In the end, I tried to give the Cookes a hint, by expressing my surprise at the total, and left them to decide what action, if any, to take.

I was slightly concerned on their behalf when they told me about more building work they had planned. They invited me in for coffee and said they were having a large enclosed porch built, even showed me architect drawings which looked rather good.

"It looks very nice, but I'd rather keep my place as it is," I said quickly, before they could try to get me involved.

"Don't blame you in some ways," Mr Cooke said. "Dealing with the planning people has been a nightmare."

"No, you're best off keeping well away from them," Mrs Cooke added. "Another custard cream?"

"I suppose you had to get lots of different quotes for the work, to be sure you were getting a good deal?" I was trying to hint they shouldn't rely on getting the best price from their builder friends.

I saw the little orange sign on the lamp post outside our houses. That surprised me as I didn't think it was required for anything as small as a porch. Somehow it seemed rude to read it with the Cookes watching, so I did it late at night when returning from work. It sounded exactly like they had described to me. When I asked at work, and gave the details I could remember I was told it was probably because they weren't using dark red bricks, which is what the rest of the house is made from. That change sounded like an improvement to me – with all the houses and garden walls being that colour, it's quite gloomy down the end of our cul-de-sac.

I didn't take up the sign's offer of viewing the plans in the council offices. Why would I, when the Cookes had already shared it with me? I didn't raise any objection either. Mostly because it didn't seem as though the work would be a problem, but partly because I'm just not the type of person to make that kind of fuss. Not without good reason.

Not long after, Mrs Cooke practically accused me of stealing a parcel she thought had been left with me. It usually is me who takes in their frequent deliveries but just for a change, I hadn't been in myself when it arrived and the driver left it with someone further down the street.

Do you think I got a whiff of an apology when she realised her mistake? No I didn't.

When the Cookes' building work started, I got rather a shock. Perhaps they hadn't lied exactly as the work at the front of the house looked exactly as in the plan they'd shown me. The back was a different matter. They hadn't mentioned anything at all about the extension their friends were building over more than half of the garden. That part was, I'm sure, deliberately withheld.

There seemed to be constant noise for months. Diggers for the foundations, cement mixers, clanging of scaffolding, hammering, drilling. It's hard for shift workers to get enough sleep at the best of times. Perhaps the dust was worse though. It seemed to get everywhere. Did I mention I'm a contract cleaner? I like the job, but that doesn't mean I want to spend all my free time doing it. Whether it was tiredness making me irritable, I can't say, but I did go round and ask the Cookes if they could possibly arrange for the noisiest work to be done in the afternoon and some kind of net screening to be put up to reduce the amount of dust blowing about.

"No one else has complained," the Cookes said.

No one else lives so close, nor needs to sleep during the day, but they somehow made me feel as though I was making more fuss than was warranted. I reminded myself that the situation was only temporary and they'd be neighbours for a long time afterwards, so did my best to smooth things over. I left with neither an apology, nor a promise of action.

They didn't apologise when one of their cars completely blocked me in either. I noticed it as I was getting ready for bed – at seven thirty, because I was on earlies that week. Going round to ask them to move it did occur to me, but I didn't want to seem to be making a fuss over nothing. I reasoned they would most likely do so that evening anyway and in the meantime it wasn't actually a problem for me.

Unfortunately it was still there when I was ready to leave for work the next morning. Five-thirty the next morning. I had to go round and ask them to move it. They called me some very rude words as they did so!

I was angry. Not just angry, absolutely furious. Yes, me. As I drove to work I couldn't help going over some previous incidents in my mind. That business with the roof for instance – maybe by getting me to pay a hefty share they'd saved themselves a lot of money and it was me and not them who'd been taken advantage of? They'd previously told the window cleaner to get the money from me and they'd settle up later, but they never got around to it and I'd never liked to say anything.

Maybe I should have looked at those plans? Now I thought about it, the windows overlooking my garden would mean I had no privacy and if their almost adult sons were going to stay living at home the parking situation would get worse. If I'd known the whole story, it's just possible I would have objected. Unlikely, but they couldn't have been sure.

They hadn't simply forgotten to tell me all the details, had they? They'd deliberately misled me and tried to put me off going in to the planning offices to learn the truth. They'd betrayed my trust. I was still fuming when I got into work. The council planning offices that night, as it happens.

Usually I keep any troubles to myself, but my colleague saw my distress and persuaded me to tell her what was wrong.

"You should teach them a lesson somehow," she said.

For once, taking action did seem like a good plan. "What do you suggest?"

"Pretend you think the extension is so great, that you're having the same done. I think that'd make them see things from your perspective a bit more." She suggested looking out their plans, photocopying them, changing the house number and dates and presenting them as my own.

"I can't do that!" Going through the council offices we clean to find potentially confidential paperwork isn't what we're paid for. Using their equipment for our own purposes is surely against a rule of some kind. And lie to the neighbours, deliberately upset them? No.

"I can!" my colleague said.

She did too. What she found was another shock. The plans submitted for approval were identical to the ones the Cookes had shown me. There was nothing at all for the extension at the back. As that was considerably larger and used the same mix of materials as the new porch, then permission should have been obtained.

"What happens to building work that's done without planning approval?" my colleague asked.

I didn't know then, but I do now. My dislike of rule breaking applies to other people as well as myself so, yes, I reported them. I've learned that in some cases unapproved work has to be put back as it was, at the owner's expense, and sometimes, if the neighbour has a good lawyer, she'll be compensated for all the inconvenience and distress she's suffered throughout the entire experience. That was also at the Cookes' expense. I do have a touch of sympathy for the fact that the cost of it all was so great they had to sell up. Sympathy, but no guilt or regret.

The Warrens live next door now. They seem fine. A bit quiet, but I don't mind that.

Not long after they moved in, a delivery lorry was parked partially over my driveway.

"I'm sorry about that," Mrs Warren said, after I'd negotiated round it to park my car after an early shift. "I hadn't realised. I'll ask him to move it."

"It's not a problem," I assured her, but only because it really wasn't, not because I'm a doormat.

Some people think I am. The Cookes next door certainly did. I'm not though. I just think it's best to stick to the rules and handle any kind of dispute quietly, and with as little fuss, as possible. Better yet, give it a chance to blow over or for someone else to sort it out without my needing to get involved at all. Might not sound much of a plan, but it often works.

3. Bad Thoughts

There was a horrible old man who thought
A lot of things that he didn't aught
Sometimes he did it out loud
In the middle of a crowd
Which is how he finally got caught

4. Romance At The Station?

Civilian admin assistant Madeleine carried a cake into the police station. As it was February 14th she'd decorated it with pink icing swirled into sugary roses. It was the first time in years Madeleine had done anything to celebrate Valentine's.

Yesterday the officers she worked with had discussed cards they'd send or receive, and dates they'd go on.

"How about you, Madeleine?" asked Sergeant Charles Winters. "Are you doing anything special?"

"I never do," she'd said.

"But it's such fun, wondering who sent you pretty things," said Constable Lindsay O'Hare. Constable Josie Garcia had nodded in agreement.

"For you two perhaps. I never receive such gifts." Madeleine instantly regretted the comment. She didn't want her colleagues to feel uncomfortable. Although single herself she didn't begrudge them romantic happiness. Hopefully the cake would prove that.

On her desk was a note. 'Madeleine everyone is in the briefing room. Please bring coffee at 9.30.' Nothing unusual about that. The same couldn't be said for the other items on her desk. Centrally placed was a large pink envelope. Top right was a little vase of flowers, top left an insulated mug decorated with love hearts, bottom left a well-filled bakery bag, bottom right a box of chocolates.

She'd have thought these were love tokens for some of the others, abandoned by her colleagues when called into the briefing room, except they were placed so precisely, and the envelope bore her name. Madeleine opened the card. Someone had written 'you're very much appreciated, Madeleine, and loved in a way that reflects the special person you are'.

Madeleine beamed. She didn't doubt she really was appreciated. So much so that someone heard what she said yesterday and today told her she was loved. Who could have done that?

She searched for clues. The flowers were daisies in the shade of burnt orange she especially liked. All her colleagues would know that, as her bag, coat, scarf and even car were that colour.

The mug held her favourite spiced latte – the drink she ordered on the odd occasion she accepted an offer from one of them to fetch her something from the coffee shop. The chocolates and cookies were favourites too – and again didn't help her guess who'd bought them as she often had some with her and always offered them to whoever was present.

Who would be most likely to have given her Valentine's gifts? Not the sergeant surely? He was divorced and closest to her own age, so in some ways seemed the most likely. But if he had any romantic interest in her he'd hidden it well up to now. It was impossible to imagine him risking embarrassing either of them by doing something so public.

Constable Micheal Ackerman often made remarks which were bordering on the flirtatious, but Madeleine was certain he didn't mean them. It was just his way of being friendly and sweet talking her into letting him have another piece of cake, or helping him with routine paperwork.

That left Detective Samuel Jones, Josie and Lindsay. They were each even less likely to be attracted to her than the sergeant or Micheal!

Madeleine hadn't narrowed down her list of suspects at all, but she was fairly confident about the motive. She was certain the gifts were meant kindly, as a sign of friendship. Were one of the young women more likely to have done such a thing than the men? Possibly, but they'd all been kind to her in different ways over the year or so she'd been working there.

Hmm, she'd picked up a few ideas about how they worked. That could help her work out who was 'guilty' of being so nice. Madeleine checked the CCTV footage of the station entrance. Detective Samuel Jones was the last to arrive and carried what could well be her mug of latte. The fact it was still piping hot supported that theory – but he often arrived carrying a drink for himself and he didn't have anything else with him. She ran the tape backwards but the only other time she saw him was when he left the previous evening.

Despite the speed with which she whizzed through the tape she realised nobody else was carrying any more than they usually did. The three constables had just their usual handbag, tiny backpack, and lunchbox, respectively. Sergeant Winters had coffee and a paper – but he'd arrived more than an hour ago, so hadn't brought her hot drink.

Madeleine made coffee for her colleagues as requested. That gave her time to puzzle out who had given her the card and gifts. When she worked it out she smiled even more widely than when she'd read the message saying she was appreciated and realised that whoever wrote those words had meant them.

Madeleine took coffee, and the Valentine's cake, into the briefing room. "I'm so glad I made this as I can say thank you to the person who gave me the card and gifts by giving them the largest piece."

The officers watched as she sliced the cake into perfectly equal slices and put each piece onto a plate.

"They're the same," Michael pointed out.

"You don't know, do you?" Josie asked.

"Oh yes I do. I watched the CCTV tape and saw that none of you brought all of those things with you today – which means you were all in it together and each brought one item."

"I told you she's as clever as she is friendly and helpful, and would work it out," Michael told the others.

"If you think flattery like that will get you one of my chocolates… you're probably right," Madeleine said.

5. Being A Mother

"Don't worry, I'll go on my own!" Maria said, not that anyone was listening. Perhaps they'd hear the door slam?

OK, she was acting like a stroppy teenager, but why not? It released some of the tension caused by her two daughters and Andy, her ex, who was the biggest kid of the lot. She'd divorced him when she'd discovered his little boy charm was directed towards a string of other women. Then, like a toddler throwing a tantrum, he'd walked out of their lives. He'd reappeared occasionally, but never for long. Now he was back in the girl's lives, for good so he said, and it looked like he'd break Maria's heart in a different way.

Trish, her oldest daughter, wasn't really a teenager, but wedding nerves made her just as emotional as she had been when suffering hormone induced mood swings during puberty. Her marriage would make such a big change – she'd be accompanying her husband on his overseas postings. Maria would miss her so much. She was trying to be upbeat about it, but Sasha, her younger daughter, wasn't helping at all.

When Maria hopefully mentioned the newlyweds visiting when on leave, Sasha reminded them about the groom's family living four hundred miles north of them and her dad Andy three hundred miles south. Then, just that morning, she'd said something which resulted in the new guest list being ripped up and the bride tearfully starting again.

When Maria tackled Sasha all she said was she hadn't meant to be mean and hadn't realised she'd upset anyone.

"Do you think you'll manage to say something nice about the clothes I try on for the wedding?" Maria had asked.

"Not if they're candyfloss pink." Sasha named the colour which had been chosen for the bouquets, bridesmaid dresses and just about everything else. OK, so it wasn't Sasha's favourite shade, but surely she could put aside her own preferences just this once? She'd been negative about all the pretty pink finishing touches Trish wanted. That's why Maria was now wandering around town on her own, in the March drizzle, half heartedly looking at mother-of-the bride outfits.

She'd counted on Sasha's help. She was studying design at college and had great dress sense. Maria sighed – Sasha was quite right that the pale pink her sister wanted wasn't a good choice for an early spring wedding, especially the frilly yet flimsy dresses, tropical flowers, and open horse drawn carriage, but her father had showed her the photos of some WAG's Californian wedding and she'd apparently set her heart on something similar. Maria hadn't been able to bring herself to say no, despite it not being likely the weather would be suitable.

Temporarily giving up on dresses and hats, Maria decided to buy a lipstick, to see if she could paint on a smile. None appealed. And the price of some of them! Who'd pay that much? Certainly not Maria, with an extravagant wedding to somehow find the money for. Originally Trish and Jason were going to have a nice lunch with just close friends and family, then a disco with a buffet afterwards, to which they'd invite all their friends, more distant relatives, and colleagues. Then Andy had reappeared, declared nothing was too good for his darling girl and promised to pay for half. At first they'd all rolled their eyes at that, but he'd explained about his new job and handed over the cost of the wedding dress to show he was serious. That forced Maria into offering to pay the other half, or look mean in comparison.

When Maria headed for home she discovered she was still holding one of the expensive lipsticks. She'd stolen it! What should she do? She shoved it in her bag until she could decide.

Only Sasha was at home.

"Where's Trish?" Maria asked her.

"She's with Jason, drawing up another guest list."

"Another one! What did you say to her this time?"

"That you can't afford a reception for 250 people, and even if you could the hotel can't seat half that many for a formal dinner, and that if she wanted to invite everyone she'd ever met, she'd have to find somewhere bigger and cheaper."

"Oh." Trish won't have liked that! As she'd said, this was the biggest day of her life and she didn't want anything small or cheap. Or had that been Andy?

"She wasn't happy," Sasha admitted.

"I'm not surprised! Why did you say it?"

"Someone had to, Mum. She had no idea how much it was all going to cost. With Dad encouraging her to make it impressive things got out of hand, but she's gone back to their original idea of lunch for a small group and a disco afterwards."

"She has?" Relief flooded through Maria. She'd not wanted to say anything which might upset Trish, but she'd been growing concerned about the spiralling costs, and that was without worrying how she'd do the same for Sasha should she want to get married before Maria had paid off the loan she was going to need.

"And she's seen sense about all the pale pink. I reminded her she's always preferred blue and that a stronger colour would mean she'd only need a few items in the right shade as 'accent' accessories at the reception and wouldn't have to drive herself and everyone else crazy trying to find everything to match and spending £12 each on getting napkins especially made."

Maria couldn't even manage one word in response. That was so much more practical, and Sasha was right; all that pink froth would have done nothing for Trish's complexion. Perhaps she should have said something…

"And she was OK about it all?" Maria asked.

"She gave me a hug before she left and said sorry for having temporarily turned into Bridezilla."

"I want to hug you too, and apologise for misjudging you. I thought you weren't being supportive of your sister."

"I was, only I was doing it in the way… Oh, never mind. Come here."

They hugged and then Sasha said, "I'll miss her too but, like I said, as we're smack in the middle of the country, between Jason's family and Dad, so this is perfect base for them whenever they can get back."

Of course Sasha would miss her sister. The girls squabbled sometimes, but had always been close; perhaps their way of making up for the dad who'd left when the youngest was just a toddler, reappearing now and again with lavish gifts. He'd give them anything they wanted – unless he'd got bored of playing the doting father before he got around to buying it, or the money ran out, or his latest girlfriend got jealous. That left Maria to explain they couldn't now have whatever it was, go where he'd said he'd take them, do the impossible things he'd made them believe would really happen. In short, to be a grown up. A responsible parent. Something she'd not felt capable of these last few days.

"What's up, Mum?"

How could she apologise for acting like a troublesome kid and leaving her youngest child to play the part of mother to her big sister?

"Come on, out with it, Mum. You looked so guilty when you came in. I know something is wrong – remember telling me you'd always know and always help?"

Maria did. After a couple of weeks of Andy buying the girls endless sweets and comics, seven-year-old Sasha had felt entitled to have what she wanted even when he wasn't around. The girls' headteacher teacher had got complaints about shoplifting and sent a note home to all the parents. As soon as Maria read it to her daughters she'd seen Sasha was guilty.

Oh! She'd completely forgotten about the lipstick. Maria held it out.

Sasha took it and twisted the end. "Yuck. What were you thinking? It's a horrible colour and won't suit you at all."

"That's hardly the point. I've just stolen it."

"Mum!"

"I didn't mean to."

"It fell into your bag did it?"

"No. This only happened because…" Maria just stopped herself from saying it was Sasha's fault for having annoyed her, or not being with her. Of course it wasn't. None of this was Sasha's fault.

"Mum, we can fix this. Remember when I nicked those sweets? You took me back and paid and I said sorry. It was all OK then and it will be this time."

"I suppose."

"If you like, we can say it was me again."

"What? No! Thanks, but I can't let you take the blame."

Sasha gave Maria a huge grin and another hug – the reaction seemed out of proportion for relief at not having to do something she'd just offered to do.

"What's that for?" Maria asked.

"Being my mum."

Before Maria could say she didn't deserve that gratitude, Sasha asked, "You're worried about seeing Dad again at the wedding, aren't you?"

"No." Finally Maria admitted the truth first to herself and then to her daughter. "It's more that I'm jealous."

Since Andy had suddenly reappeared, he'd given the girls gifts and attention, praised them and made them laugh. Maria couldn't blame the girls for falling for his irresistible charm. She'd once done the same. Neither could she blame Andy for wanting to get to know his wonderful daughters, but she wouldn't let him take her place in their hearts.

"He's not the one who's had to say no to you both over the years and now he turns up acting like your new best friend and I can't compete," Maria said.

"No, you can't."

"Thanks a lot!"

"I promised to always tell you the truth, didn't I, after you caught me stealing? That honesty is one of the reasons you wanted me to come when you pick your wedding outfit?"

"True."

"So, listen to me now. Just be our mum, OK? That's what we need. Not someone letting me eat pizza and ice cream every night, or letting me stay out way too late, or agreeing to crazy wedding plans because you don't want to be unpopular. We don't want you to try being a better friend to us than Dad. Not that it would be hard as he's not exactly reliable is he?"

"When your father and I split up, I promised I'd not speak against him to either of you."

She'd been tempted though, when she heard of the promises he'd made. Maria knew all to well that although he might mean them at the time, they were often beyond his control, or pocket, or attention span. He said what he thought people wanted to hear, believed it himself, and blamed someone else when it went wrong. That's not how a father should behave. Nor a mother.

Sasha was right. Maria had been so busy trying to compete with Andy, she'd forgotten her role as a mother. Someone to set boundaries and offer guidance. Someone who'd do what was best for them, even if it was difficult. Who accepted her responsibilities.

Maria went into the shop she'd accidentally stolen from on her own. Returning the lipstick was embarrassing, but it was the proper grown-up thing to do. Once that was over, Sasha and Trish helped Maria choose a suitable, and not too expensive, blue dress to wear at Trish's wedding. Then the three of them giggled like schoolgirls as they both tried on totally unsuitable hats.

Well, mums should be fun too – shouldn't they?

6. Toxic

I remember the first time I met Peter and I wish I'd known then what I know now. It was quite a big deal, us meeting him. Joanna had told us so much about him but this was the first time she'd persuaded him to come and meet 'the parents'. I'd got myself into a bit of a state about it. Silly I know. It should have been him on approval to see if he was good enough for our darling daughter, yet I found myself desperate to make a good impression.

I'd heard so much about his exotic life travelling all over the world that I decided to make paella – a dish I'd never attempted before. I bought the ingredients well in advance and had a practise so hadn't completely taken leave of my senses. Then Joanna called on the morning to say he couldn't make Sunday lunch after all. Some business problem of Peter's. I should have been suspicious then, I suppose.

Anyway, he didn't come until Friday and by then the seafood had gone a funny colour and smelled… Actually, I don't choose to remember how it smelled. I made a cottage pie. That seemed to go down well.

Since then, Peter has let down our lovely Joanna, time after time. We learnt why when his wife turned up. That's the wife in Spain. She tracked down his English wife and the French one.

I wished I'd known that rancid seafood is toxic. I'd have fed him the lot.

7. It's Not Fair!

"I can't eat that. I'm vegetarian," Paul's ten-year-old daughter informed me.

My irritation probably showed. Don't get me wrong, I respect the compassion of people who choose not to eat meat. Martha's ethics however seemed a little shaky.

Less than four hours previously she'd sulked in the supermarket when, after reading the ingredients and declaring them to be concoction of salt, palm oil, colouring, flavours, sweeteners and reformed turkey scraps, I refused to buy Flamingo Frazzlers. She hadn't been impressed when I added broccoli, red cabbage and swede to the trolley either.

She pushed the healthy meal round her plate. "I want something else."

"You can have dessert, but only if you finish your main course. You know the rule."

"But…"

"Not the meat of course, as you're a vegetarian." Using my fork, I speared the juicy pork chop from her plate and transferred it to mine.

"You have to make me something else."

"No. I don't." I continued eating.

"I'll tell Dad."

"Not until after dinner. You know the rule; no phones during a meal."

I was confident she'd stay at the table. She'd helped mix the sticky toffee pudding which wafted tempting caramel aromas from the oven.

"It's not fair," she wailed. "Those are Mum's rules!"

I understood her frustration. In the past I've taken Martha to exciting places, bought lavish gifts, given in to her sudden whims and been generally overindulgent. When she's not being stroppy she's adorable and I've long wished she were mine. Besides, she's the apple of her father's eye and winning her affection guarantees gaining his.

Paul and I have been friends since school. Sometimes, whilst growing up, I wished we were more than friends and there were a couple of occasions when we… Let's just say we got extra close.

By the time Paul met Fiona, I was with Dale so I wasn't jealous. Not really. I became friends with her and the four of us socialised together quite a lot until Fiona fell pregnant. Then it was usually just Paul, Dale and myself. Ironically that's when my jealousy kicked in. Fiona seemed to have it all.

At the risk of sounding like Martha, I didn't think it was fair. I couldn't have children, Dale showed no interest in putting a ring on my finger and, well, he wasn't Paul. Not sure whether it was the unfavourable comparisons, or my increasingly desperate attempts to conceive, but eventually Dale dumped me.

Paul comforted me and shared the rum I'd opened; probably to stop me drinking the entire bottle. I was too distraught to intend anything that night, but when I awoke in Paul's arms the next morning, I planned to make that a regular occurrence.

I timed my confession to Fiona, for the night spent with her husband, perfectly. She'd just had a disastrous haircut, Martha had stormed upstairs in a strop and Paul had been away on business yet again. Despite me providing some intimate details and the revelation our earlier relationship wasn't entirely innocent, I was surprised how easily Fiona was convinced. Can't have been much of a marriage with so little trust, can it?

When she told him to go, I thought he'd come to me. Instead he went to a hotel, but not until he'd sworn to her nothing had happened that night and he really had been working the previous weekend. Fiona was icy calm with me, but apparently not with him. Martha overheard and took her father's side, blaming Fiona for the split and claiming to hate her mother. I discovered all this when the kid arrived on my doorstep, saying she'd run away.

Seizing my chance, I offered Martha a place in my home as well as my heart. I was fairly confident that where Martha went, Paul would soon follow.

For a couple of hours we had huge fun. We went to the pictures, with me buying about three pounds of pick and mix sweets on the way in. During the cartoon I decided bedtime would be as late as she liked and I promised to buy her a computer tablet of her own, despite Fiona having made it clear she felt Martha was far too young for unrestricted internet access. We bought ice cream on the way out.

"You're brilliant," Martha declared. "Mum hardly lets me have anything with sugar in it."

Now, I do sometimes think Fiona is a bit strict with Martha, but with all the dire warnings about childhood obesity, tooth decay and the rise in diabetes, I could see where she was coming from on that one. It was only natural she worried about her daughter's health.

That's when it began to hit me that I might have made a mistake. There's a world of difference between taking a child out for the day and taking her on full time. All right then, two mistakes. Obviously Martha's absence would be of concern to her mother. In fact Fiona must be worried sick. Perhaps even worried enough to call the police.

"You'd better phone your mum and tell her you're OK," I said.

"Do I have to? She'll yell at me."

"Pass her over to me if she does."

I watched a range of emotions flit over Martha's face. I realised that despite saying she hated Fiona and much preferred being with me, it wasn't quite as simple as that. From what I could make out Fiona didn't yell at her daughter, but I was still handed the phone. There was plenty of yelling then as well as some very choice words. I didn't dare move the phone away from my ear in case Martha heard.

Once Fiona ran out of steam I said, "I didn't kidnap her, or even invite her. Martha came to me because she was miserable at home."

After being informed, at length, that the misery was entirely my fault, I said, "You know I love Martha and wouldn't do anything to hurt her. Not deliberately anyway," I added because I saw she did sort of have a point. "She's welcome to stay with me as long as she wants, but I certainly won't try to make her stay anywhere she doesn't want to be." I cut Fiona off, just in case she was able to think of a suitable reply.

Paul called me soon afterwards.

"Thank you for looking after Martha. I've no idea what's got into Fiona, but she seems to think we've been having an affair, and seeing us rowing has been hard on the poor kid."

"So I understand. Don't worry, I'll cheer her up and I can cut my hours at work a bit so I can take her to school and pick her up again no problem, and of course you can come and see her anytime."

"I think we'd better keep our distance for a while," he said. He also reminded me that children need boundaries.

By then I'd started to realise that if I was going to have responsibility of her for more than the odd day, constantly spoiling her in an effort to win her affection away from Fiona wasn't really in Martha's best interests. Reluctantly I agreed to implement the rules her parents had jointly set.

Doing the right thing can be hard, can't it? It would have been so easy to give in to her every whim, but I resisted.

"Right, we'd better go shopping then," I'd said once she'd said goodbye to Paul.

"For my tablet?"

"No. For food. We can't live on ice cream, can we?"

She agreed with that, but we didn't entirely see eye to eye on suitable alternatives. The sulk over my refusal to buy Flamingo Frazzlers returned not long after we got back from shopping and I declared that she couldn't play her educational computer game.

"I don't have that child lock thing on my computer, so you can only use it when I'm sitting with you, and right now I want to watch the news."

"But that's boring!"

"Watch anyway. You might learn something."

My failure to cook a replacement meal when she turned her nose up at the chop didn't get a huge reaction. However she had a mini meltdown when I insisted she help wash up before watching TV and so missed half of her favourite programme.

I weakened a bit and said she could watch it on iPlayer. We played games until it was available and had hot chocolate afterwards which meant she got to stay up quite late. I tried to make up for that by giving her grapefruit for breakfast and insisting she do her homework before we did anything else. As she was already annoyed with me I decided I might as well get all the other unpleasant stuff out the way and explained that in future bedtimes would be earlier, sugary foods rationed and TV viewing restricted.

"I want to go back to Mum's."

"She'll say the same."

"I know, but she's my mum. It's her job to tell me what to do."

Unable to argue with that, I said, "Better go and collect up your stuff then, hadn't you?" I'd gambled my friendship with Paul's wife and a role in her daughter's life for the chance to have him and Martha for myself. Gambled and lost it seemed, but there was still one thing I could do.

With Martha out the way, I rang Fiona and told her not only that she could collect her daughter, but the truth.

"Paul and I didn't ever have any kind of affair. I wildly exaggerated what happened when we were kids and implied a whole lot more had gone on since since. Paul only stayed that night because he fell asleep and I only know about his birthmark because he told me, not because I've seen it."

"I know. We'll both be coming to collect Martha. Please have her ready to come out, as I intend this to be the last time either of us speak to you."

Her tone was overly harsh, I thought. But then she didn't know what I'd left out of my confession. I knew being strict with Martha, after my earlier indulgence, would alienate her. I lied about most of the ingredients in the Flamingo Frazzlers and knew her parents would have let her eat them. Then I made certain she saw that news report on intensively reared pork just as our meal was cooking. I had it on a low setting to be sure she'd miss the start of the programme she was so desperate to watch. I also knew that worry over Martha would get Fiona and Paul talking and the discussions would progress better without Martha there getting upset and taking sides.

I doubt any of them will forgive me for trying to rip their family apart. Neither will I get any credit for helping put it back together. I had to do it though. When you love someone you have to do what's best for them don't you? You see, much as I've always liked Paul, it's Martha I really love and who I wanted to fill the emptiness of my childless life. It's her happiness which is more important than my own.

8. Hey, That Was Mine!

"Hey, that was mine!" I told Louise as she grabbed the biggest slice of pizza, and a chunk of garlic sausage which clearly belonged to the remaining slice.

"Oh, was it?" she asked with fake innocence and ate it anyway.

I wasn't surprised as she'd been taking what was mine since the day we met. That was over fifteen years ago and I wasn't putting up with it a day longer!

I disappeared into the kitchen, where I made a jug of pina colada with extra rum. I poured equal quantities into huge glasses, then added a little extra to Louise's. I decorated each with a piece of fresh pineapple wedged onto the rim of the glass, and a cocktail stick threaded with glacé cherries balanced on top. I used three cherries for mine and five for hers.

"They look fantastic, Sarah!" Louise said, as I put the fuller one in front of her.

I picked up my own glass, before she could even consider reaching for it, and swallowed a mouthful. "They taste it too!"

As Louise took a sip of hers I excused myself, saying I needed the loo. Truth was I could no longer look my friend in the face. Former friend. She didn't know it yet, but the drink was the last thing she would take from me – willingly or otherwise.

To be fair to her, taking what was mine wasn't always deliberate. She was the new girl at school and couldn't have known the bus seat she'd occupied was the one I thought of as mine. When I explained she asked if we could sit together. I agreed and she took that to mean we were friends. That would have been OK, but she took on all my other friends too. She had novelty value and I felt pushed aside.

She came round the house a lot, where she ate most of the snacks Mum made for me and somehow often left with one of my toys, or wearing something of mine. As we got older she 'borrowed' a lot of my clothes. It was kind of flattering in a way, to see she admired my taste so much, but it was annoying too.

"You can wear something of mine," she'd say when we were at hers getting ready for a party and she'd put on the dress I'd brought to wear. She's always been a size smaller than me.

Of course she got the boys I felt should have been mine – partly because it took away my confidence to have Louise, a slimmer version of myself, constantly by my side. She even took a job away from me. My fault for telling her how perfect it sounded and making her think she'd love it too. Oh, she claimed she'd applied in the hope of us working together, but as I knew only one position was available, I'm sure she did too.

Actually I eventually took that job from her – when she got promoted. On Valentine's day, which was only a week after I started, she took the anonymous bouquet left on my desk, saying whoever left them couldn't have realised she now had her own office.

About the only thing Louise doesn't often take is the hints I've given about the error of her ways. Usually she ignores my complaints. Sometimes she attempts to make it up to me, but she doesn't try very hard or very often.

One time she 'borrowed' one of my dresses and I 'forgot' to tell her I'd somehow got bits of rose hip on it so wearing it would make her itch horribly. She was still a bit sore after having it dry cleaned for me! Occasionally, when I've made my annoyance clear, she apologises, but she doesn't stop.

This morning I got to work and found her car in my parking space. No doubt she'd have a plausible excuse, but it was the final straw. At lunchtime I went out and bought that little extra which I added to her cocktail, then I went to her office and invited her for a drink this evening.

I can't hide in the loo all night. I have to get Louise outside, so her body is found well away from my flat.

She's downed half her drink – more than enough for my purposes. And she's eaten my cherries as well as hers. True to form, right to the end!

I hastily finish my pina colada. "Gosh, that's strong. Shall we take a walk to clear our heads?" I suggest.

"Good idea. But not in these shoes. I'll wear your trainers. You finish your drink while I find them."

"I already have, look." I show her the glass thinking that if she can't see it's empty, what I've given her is taking effect more quickly than I'd anticipated.

She shakes her head. "No, the one you drank is mine. Sorry but, as you know, sometimes I just can't help taking what's yours."

9. Learning To Manage People

Karen felt herself respond to Gary's warm smile. That attractive young man made her distasteful job in the factory bearable. He was the new shift manager and at first the women had been wary of having him in charge. They'd soon warmed to his pleasant manner, even Marjorie who'd been there for years and stood in for the previous manager whenever he was ill, or on holiday. Marjorie, and many of the others, had assumed she'd take the position when her predecessor retired but Gary had been appointed without her even being considered.

Gary had soon won her round by asking Marjorie to train him and negotiating extra pay for her while she did. He made it clear he appreciated her years of experience. He showed he appreciated Karen's efforts too by thanking her for doing a good job even when she'd done no more than her regular duties, by greeting her in the morning and asking how she was, by listening when she spoke. By treating her like a human being in fact.

She responded like one too. And she'd responded like a woman to his tall, slim frame, his thick dark brown curls and even darker eyes which sparkled with humour. She'd not got it into her head to run off with him or anything daft. For one thing he was half her age. He didn't single her out for special treatment, but was pleasant to all the women. Oh, and she was married of course.

Gary's behaviour was easy to explain; he was a decent person doing his job well. Harder to explain was why Karen was so desperate for a crumb of affection, or why she was doing a job she disliked. She understood the other women doing so; they needed the money. Her case was different. Taking the job was a favour to her brother-in-law. Karen wasn't happy to find her husband, Oscar, had agreed to the plan without consulting her. Even less pleased to find her role was that of an industrial spy. Productivity was down, sickness was up and David suspected theft. Karen was to pose as a new member of staff and find out what was going on.

"I don't want to work in a factory and I like the idea of lying to the other women even less," she told Oscar.

"I've said you would now, we can't let David down. Anyway, it's not lying, just not telling them things they don't need to know. Besides, it isn't as though you do anything important with your mornings. You mostly just drink coffee don't you?"

Not important to him maybe, but the few hours she spent sharing a coffee and chat with an elderly neighbour, an old school friend whose ill health made it difficult for her to get out much and then there was Vivian… Well, it was important to her and by cancelling she'd be letting them down. Karen thought Oscar suspected her of doing more than that; of an affair even. His first wife had been unfaithful and Karen got so annoyed by Oscar's questioning and not seeing she was different that she'd let him go on thinking it.

Karen had never been unfaithful and it wasn't through lack of opportunity. Not long after the shine was beginning to wear off her marriage and new situation, she'd bumped into Vivian, one of her former boyfriends. He'd lost none of his charm nor, it seemed, any of his interest in her. He flirted shamelessly and made it clear he'd like to do much more. She refused of course, every time. She allowed him to keep asking though, even though it was playing with fire. Once a month or so she'd meet him for lunch, a trip on the river, or visit to a garden. Not once did she go to his home or a hotel; the temptation to give in to his suggestions would have been too strong.

Knowing she wouldn't be able to meet Vivian so frequently was another reason for not wanting to take the job. She didn't want an argument though and reluctantly started work on the factory floor.

Karen promised herself she wouldn't lie to her colleagues. Just as when she'd met her former lover she told Oscar she'd been with an old school friend called Vivian, when the women asked her where she lived she'd told them the truth. When they asked where she got her shoes or had her hair done she told them. Each time they roared with laughter.

"That'll teach us to be nosey!"

"No really, it's true. That bag is a Givenchy and these shoes are Louboutin." She realised either item cost as much as her colleagues earned in a month and was far less practical than anything they had. She fully deserved to be laughed at.

"And I bet you buy all your food from Marks and Spencers?"

"A high street shop where I'd have to queue up? I don't think so! Everything is delivered by specialist suppliers."

She kept then entertained through every tea break just by telling the truth about the plays she went to, the dinner parties she hosted and the car she drove.

"Got you! I've seen you being dropped off in the mornings. By one of the bosses I think, because he parks in the executive section. What's the story there?"

"OK, I'll come clean. It's not just coincidence my surname is the same as that of the company, my husband's family own it. My brother-in-law is CEO and, as he lives next door to us, he drops me off in the mornings."

"And you get the bus home?"

"Taxi into town for lunch at Luigi's actually."

They'd laughed until their mascara ran down their faces and Karen almost envied them. They didn't have a lot, but they seemed happy. At least they did now Gary was in charge.

The work wasn't too demanding, mentally or physically, but it was the kind of fiddly task which required observation and was unsuitable for mechanisation. She hated the boring monotony of the work and of course she was treated just like everyone else so as not to arouse suspicion. That treatment was pretty awful to start with; worse than machines really. At least those got some maintenance and regular checks to see they were electrically sound.

When Karen suggested the staff should be treated with a little more respect, her brother-in-law just said, "I pay them, don't I?"

Yes, the very least he could get away with. That perhaps was just good business practice; with so many people out of work he had no trouble attracting or keeping staff. They were good women though, they should be valued, which reminded her. "I'm sure no one is stealing anything, David."

"Stuff is definitely missing."

"Well, it isn't any of the women on my shift, I've watched them."

"They must hide it in their handbags."

Oh right, she was too stupid to think they might not actually walk out with it in plain sight? He was so like his brother. When Karen suggested he show some appreciation for her he'd said, "I married you didn't I?" He'd said it in a jokey way and added, "And I get you a nice anniversary present each year."

He did too, but being reminded of that just made her think of her colleagues doing a job they didn't like in return for the money. It wasn't just the luxurious lifestyle which had persuaded her to accept Oscar's proposal. He'd got used to money being the answer to most of life's problems, that was all. Underneath he was nice man. He gave generously to charity. The gifts he gave her weren't just costly, but thoughtfully chosen and he remembered to give them to her on her birthday and their anniversary. Oscar took her out to expensive events because he knew she'd enjoy them and he wanted to show off the wife he was proud of, not just display his wealth and good taste to others in a similar situation.

When he'd agreed to her working at the factory it was because of a genuine wish to help his brother and in the knowledge she had the time to spare. He must too have thought she had the intelligence to spot whatever the problems were. So must David, or he'd not have agreed to the scheme. He wasn't really so different from Oscar. If she talked to him maybe she could get him to understand.

She was too late to suggest he give the shift manager post to Marjorie, but she did tell him there was some resentment that he'd favoured an unknown college boy over someone who'd been a loyal employee for years.

"I'm not sure one of the women could do the job."

"She was doing it unofficially before Gary started."

"Not particularly well though."

"It can't be easy when you know you're just filling in and don't have the support of management. You wouldn't have let her make any changes, would you?" She asked that knowing Marjorie had made a few suggestions and been ignored each time.

"I do see your point, Karen but I've filled the position now."

Gary had soon sized up the situation. As well as extra pay for Marjorie during the handover period he'd had it officially confirmed she was his deputy and would do his job in his absence at the same rate he got, not just the slight increase she'd been given in the past.

"I won't be here forever you know and I'll do my best to see Marjorie gets the post afterwards."

"Why are you here?" the women had asked.

"I'm learning business management at college and this is the kind of business I'll be running."

"Sure of yourself, aren't you?"

"Er, yes." He gave a cheeky grin.

Soon everyone was much happier at work. Gary gave rewards whenever targets were met. Nothing much, often just star stickers on a chart, but it was a rare day they didn't earn them.

"Waste of time," David said when Karen first reported back.

"But it's working. Targets are almost always met now."

"If they can do it now they should have before."

"They needed encouragement and praise. If someone has worked hard then a word of thanks makes them feel it was worth the effort. If it seems their efforts weren't appreciated or even noticed then why push themselves?"

"Right." David didn't look fully convinced, but she noticed Oscar nodding his head.

The three of them fell silent as they ate the shop bought meal she'd warmed up. Unless it was a special dinner party, neither her husband nor David, who was a regular dinner guest, ever thanked her for the hours she spent preparing them imaginative meals. So instead of bothering she used her afternoons for the visits she used to make each morning and did the minimum she could towards providing an evening meal.

On Sunday though she made a proper roast dinner, including stuffing flavoured with fresh herbs, wine-enriched gravy and glazed vegetables. She followed that with a buttery fruit crumble and creamy custard. Oscar was lavish with praise.

"It's just what I always made, when I had time."

"And it was always delicious. Sorry I didn't say before, love."

"Me too, Karen," David said. "The food you so generously share with me is always superb. I've rather taken you for granted."

"Yes, you have. Still, I see you're both starting to learn your lesson, so how about I make that coffee torte you both like so much? It should be ready by the time you've had a round of golf."

The brothers went off in good spirits, but not until after they'd carried their used crockery through into the kitchen and offered to wash up. They looked relieved when she said no, but at least they'd thought to ask.

A week later, David discovered it was some of the warehouse staff who were responsible for the thefts. They'd loaded more than they should onto some lorries and split the profits with the drivers. An innocent colleague had realised what was happening and reported them.

"You were right, Karen," he said over dinner. "The women you work with had nothing to do with it and I had no reason to suspect them."

"So what are you going to do?"

"I've sacked the guilty ones and reported them to the police, naturally. I'll have to make sure there are better checks on the others and they have no opportunity to do the same thing."

"Or you could show you appreciate their loyalty by not getting involved in the scam and being brave enough to tell you about it? And perhaps treat them decently in future so they want to remain loyal?"

David started to speak, then sipped his wine and looked thoughtful. "Fair point. If they were all as bad as each other it would have been a long time before I'd worked out what was happening."

Karen wasn't sure David had fully understood the point she was trying to make, but it seemed Oscar had. The way he asked about her day changed. He stopped asking, 'where did you go?', 'who did you speak to?' as though she needed an alibi. Instead he asked if Doris's leg was any better and if she'd had fun with her friends, making it at least sound as though he knew that's who she'd been with and cared about how she felt. "And how is Vivian?"

"Fine I'm sure, but I've not seen Vivian for quite a while now."

"You've been too busy?"

"Not just that, I prefer other people's company these days." People she had no reason to feel guilty for spending time with.

Just as things started to improve at home, it seemed they were to get worse at work. Gary called the women together and told them he was leaving. Along with all the "We'll miss you," and "Good luck at your next job," comments there were also a few remarks along the lines of, "Soon you'll be a manager yourself," and "Will you have jobs for us?"

David of course knew Gary was leaving and honoured his promise that Marjorie be considered to take his place and gave her the job on a trial basis.

"And you'll give her the support she needs to succeed?" Karen prompted.

"Er, yes. Do you think she'll need much?"

Worried the woman wouldn't get the chance to prove herself, Karen rather exaggerated the changes which might result from Gary leaving. "She will if a lot of people leave."

"Why would they?"

"You do know Gary's course is almost finished and he's been conditionally accepted for a rival company. I forget the name, but I don't suppose the rest of my shift have. Gary was very popular, so they'd be happy to work for him and of course he knows who all the best workers are."

"What should I do?"

"You got me in to advise you, but you've not listened to a word I've said, have you?"

Oscar said, "He might not, but I certainly have."

"I know, love." She kissed him. "Explain it to your brother will you, I need to check on dinner."

The following Monday, Marjorie was all smiles as she returned from a management meeting. "I've been given a new contract and officially confirmed as your permanent shift manager."

She was warmly congratulated.

"Well I'd better get on with the job," she said when she could get in a word. "My first task is to pass on a message from our Karen's brother, the big boss himself."

Their groans almost drowned out Karen's comment of, "He's my brother-in-law actually."

"Don't be like that," Marjorie said. "He actually wanted me to pass on his thanks that we're all meeting our targets, despite a change of management which he understands might have been unsettling, and to keep up the good work."

"David said that?" Karen gasped.

"Yes, he really did. Could it be you don't know him quite as well as you led us to believe?" she asked with a grin.

"It would seem so."

Karen had a further surprise when David, carrying a large box, strode onto the factory floor half way through Friday's shift and asked them to stop work. Everyone apart from Marjorie looked as shocked as Karen felt.

"Well done, ladies," he said. "Marjorie tells me you've already exceeded this week's target. I've brought you these as a reward." He opened the box to reveal a selection of enticing looking cakes.

As the women made their selection, David asked Karen if that met with her approval.

"Indeed it does, but if you're going to make a habit of treating them every time they exceed targets, can I suggest a basket of fruit? That's healthier and you do want your staff to be healthy."

"Good point, thanks and well, thanks for everything else too." He kissed her cheek.

They stepped apart and saw the others were staring at them. "I did say he's my brother-in-law," she pointed out.

After a few seconds of quiet, one woman asked, "So those shoes you lent me for my sister's wedding really were those Loubo whatsits and worth hundreds of quid?"

"Er, yes."

"And the bag you let me have is a real Armani one?" asked someone else.

"Last season's and scuffed, but yes."

After that of course it was impossible for Karen to continue in her job. Instead she called in about once a month as a kind of welfare officer. When staff were off sick she visited to check if they had all they needed. She chatted with the women and listened to their work related concerns, of which there were few.

Otherwise her life went back to normal. Or almost. She told Vivian, quite truthfully, that she no longer had room in her life for him. Karen no longer felt taken for granted or unappreciated by Oscar and she showed her appreciation of him in several ways, some involving cookery and all putting a smile on his face. A smile she responded to.

10. Parting Gift

"This is from all of us," a colleague from Akadri Accounts said, handing me a gift-wrapped basket.

Five years I'd been there and not one of them knew me well enough to come up with something better than toiletries. As much my fault as theirs. I'm a private person. Not unfriendly – I'm always ready for a chat, and often join my colleagues for a drink after work, but find it incredibly hard to open up.

The only person I'd revealed any of my inner self to was my boss, Craig Akadri. I hadn't gone so crazy as to tell him I loved him, although I did. I'd just explained why I wanted time off in March. For accountants that's the busiest time, so you need a good reason.

"My great-grandad was William Carmichael," I told him.

"The artist?"

I was surprised he knew the name. Great-grandad's paintings are quite valuable now, but still not widely known.

I told Craig how much I wanted to see another of my ancestor's paintings for real. "Most are in private collections. Those on public display are spread around America. I saw one in a gallery on my last holiday." After that I'd decided not to spend more money viewing others, but save it and pursue my dream of becoming a painter myself. I'd taken evening classes and dabbled at the weekends. The results were quite good, but I really needed more lessons, and more time in which to work on my art.

"And you want to see others. I understand, Shona, but you can do that any time of year, can't you?"

"Those in galleries, yes, but someone has found what they think is another one, although it's unsigned. It's believed to be of William's sister. I've seen sketches he did of her, when he was young, so I'll know if it's really his."

"If you're able to declare it as genuine the value will rise considerably. I'm sure it's owner would wait a week or two for that."

"The owner has died and his estate is up for auction. The only way, and only time, I can see it is at the sale." I told him I'd asked to see it before, explaining my reason, but got a very curt dismissal in return. "The man it belonged to is apparently a very distant relation. That makes it more likely to be genuine, but also made them suspicious I was trying to make a claim." No doubt I said a lot more. When talking to Craig I either clam up completely or babble inanely.

He'd agreed I could go. I'd thought he was being kind.

The painting was by my great-grandad, I was certain. Not only did the subject look exactly like the girl in the sketches of his which I owned, but the pose and scenery also matched. With the provenance I had, the painting would be worth hundreds of thousands. Without it… maybe it would be cheap enough for me to buy. That would give me a dilemma – to keep it, or sell it on in the hope I'd eventually produce more of my own.

The auctioneer suggested a low opening bid. Nobody responded, so he named an even lower amount. I held my nerve until he went lower still, then raised my hand.

The auctioneer repeated my bid and invited a higher one. It was slow to come and only fifty pounds more. I raised my hand again. My opponent shook his head.

"Are we all out?" the auctioneer asked. He raised his gavel. "Going, going…"

"Here!" a man called from the back.

I bid against him. He countered every time, even when I lost control and bid more than I could ever pay. Eventually I stopped and was relieved to be outbid. The painting would never be mine, but I was saved the humiliation of confessing I didn't have the money.

Despite my jealousy that he now owned great-grandfather's painting, I had a little sympathy for the man who'd paid much more than he would have, had it not been for my recklessness. I followed, intending to tell him he actually had a bargain.

I overheard his call. "I've got it, Mr Akadri."

I felt sick. Akadri isn't a common surname. There'd been very little interest in that painting. No one would have bid so high unless they had good reason to believe it to be a genuine William Carmichael, and by bidding myself I'd confirmed to Craig's hired hand that's what it was.

I'd confided in Craig and he'd used it against me. I've never been so hurt, nor so angry.

My notice was written before I returned to work. As with all accountants, the end of the financial year meant I'd been working extra hours and was therefore owed time off. That cut my month's notice down to two weeks. Craig was obviously unhappy, but he arranged I'd get the annual bonus which wasn't due to be paid until summer. Motivated by guilt no doubt.

"We also got you these," another colleague said. The gorgeous bouquet she held brought me back to the present. "We know how much you like flowers."

There was a card too, with messages from everyone. Craig's 'you'll be greatly missed' didn't mean much, but some others did. There were reminders of funny incidents we'd shared, good wishes for the future which suggested they cared more than I'd realised. That was kind considering I'd left everyone in the lurch.

Of course they'd not had time to buy me a more appropriate gift. With just two weeks to do it, and everyone working overtime, it was amazing they'd managed to pass round an envelope, let alone spend the contents.

"Shona, may I have a word?" Craig asked.

I nodded and followed him to his office. My leaving so abruptly really hadn't been fair on him. I'd told myself that buying the painting wasn't fair to me, in an attempt to extinguish my unrequited love, but it wasn't true. I hadn't told him I hoped to buy it – just that the sale was my one and only chance to see it.

I was ready to provide him with proof his purchase was worth more than he'd paid, until I saw great-grandad's painting leaning against his desk, criss-crossed in shiny ribbon.

"I bought it intending to hang it there," he indicated the wall opposite. "I thought it might encourage you to spend more time in here."

I had to ask him to repeat that.

He did, adding, "As that's failed, I'd like you to have it. Maybe it will inspire your own painting."

When had I told him about that? Why had he remembered?

"Or perhaps you'll need to sell it in order to fund your studies and early work. In which case, I'll be happy to buy it back at its true value."

"But why?" I asked.

"To hang it here, so that you may come and see it whenever you wish."

I walked straight out of Craig's office – to tell my colleagues I was staying until all the tax returns were filed. I never did leave for good, as I return frequently to where the painting, and my love, are waiting for me.

11. Stop Thief!

Sue smiled as she made her lunch plan. She was a little nervous, but also full of optimism. If things went well on Sunday then it could be the start of a really good relationship. Tom, her son, was bringing his girlfriend Jessica to meet Sue for the first time.

When she'd first heard the girl's name Sue hadn't been at all enthusiastic – that's what both the annoying assistant at her dentist and a particularly unpleasant former colleague were called. Of course Jessica was a very popular name for young women and from what Tom had said, and he often did talk about her, his Jessica was perfectly lovely. By the time her son suggested bringing her for lunch, Sue was sure that this Jessica would become her daughter-in-law and that they'd get on very well.

On Sue's shopping list was a nice joint of lamb. It was a favourite of hers and something she knew she could cook well – and she'd checked Jessica wasn't vegetarian or allergic to anything. Although red wine would be traditional with the dark meat, that seemed too heavy for daytime. Sue decided on a bottle of Cava. That was lighter and this felt like a special occasion, so something bubbly seemed appropriate.

For dessert they were having trifle. That was Tom's favourite and she could make it well in advance. Sue added cream, strawberries and sponge fingers to her list. Should they have a starter?

She rang Tom to ask if Jessica had a favourite food.

"She's very fond of smoked salmon, but honestly, Mum, you don't need to go to any trouble. I just want you two to meet properly and be friends."

"I'll go to as much trouble as I like!" she joked. Then, as she registered all of his words, added, "What do you mean by 'meet properly'? Have I come across Jessica before?" Oh dear, the girl from the dentist? But maybe Sue had been unfair to her and her super upbeat manner wasn't half so annoying if you weren't just about to have your teeth drilled.

"Yeah. I forgot to mention it as it didn't seem important."

"Tell me now then."

"I think she replaced you at McIver's."

"She's Jessica Brown?" No, it couldn't be. Tom couldn't have fallen in love with anyone so awful…

"That's right. See you Sunday!"

All the humiliation Sue had suffered due to that girl came flooding back. Jessica wasn't Sue's direct replacement, it was just coincidence she'd decided to hand in her notice the week the girl started. As Sue had holiday time to take they only overlapped for a few days, but it was more than enough to have a horrible impact.

Two days before Sue left, she learned toilet rolls had gone missing from the cleaner's supply cupboard. The boss had sent round a memo about it, saying steps were being taken to find the culprit, who would be dealt with to the fullest extent the law allowed. The theft might sound trivial, but it was almost fifty pound's worth and, more to the point, everyone should be able to trust everyone else.

When Sue had attempted to drive out the car park that evening, the barrier hadn't risen for her. The two security staff approached her.

"Could you open the boot of your car, please?" one asked.

As soon as he spoke, Sue got a sick feeling in her stomach. She knew what they'd see and what they'd no doubt think. She did as they requested and stood aside to let them see the toilet rolls. She'd bought several packs as they'd been on offer and it looked more because under them were a range of sanitary items, all to be donated to a local woman's shelter.

Sue scrabbled in her bag for the receipt. The security guards quickly realised Sue was no thief, but not before several colleagues had gone slowly past, taking a good look at her predicament and the huge selection of rather personal items. She'd been so embarrassed she probably looked guilty. When she was told she could go she was shaking so much she'd had to go for a coffee before feeling able to drive home.

When she drove in the next morning, her final day at McIver's, she was handed a note asking her to go straight to the manager's office. The boss said she knew Sue had done nothing wrong and explained someone had noticed Sue leave a little early, watched as she put the photos she'd cleared from her desk into the boot and seen the toilet rolls.

"She notified me and I called security to have you stopped. Sorry, but I had no choice."

Yes she did. The boss could have trusted her. Sue had worked there for years and the boss knew about her voluntary work in the shelter as she'd given her permission to leave a little earlier on Tuesdays if she was up to date with everything. But she'd had her stopped because Jessica Brown jumped to the conclusion Sue was a thief. It had to have been her as nobody but the new girl would have been surprised by Sue leaving ten minutes early on a Tuesday.

Sue went to a washroom to compose herself and overheard two women gossiping about her being stopped the previous afternoon. Oh no! When people discovered she'd left the very next day they'd all believe she was guilty and had been sacked because of it. She felt so upset and ashamed she just wanted to go home, but then even those she worked closely with might suspect her.

When she'd reached her own desk, Jessica had tried to apologise for her mistake. Sue didn't dare say anything – if she had she'd have caused a scene which would be another black mark on people's memory of her. Instead she'd started opening the pile of leaving cards on her desk. They contained sweet messages and everyone had clubbed together for a thoughtful gift and luscious selection of cakes. It should have been a special day.

"It's all been spoiled," she confided to one of her friends. "I feel my whole time here has been tainted by that accusation."

"Don't overreact, Sue. It was just a mistake."

It was clear the incident had been discussed in Sue's absence and everyone felt Jessica had been right to act as she had.

That had been two years ago. She now had a job she loved and had tried to put it behind her. She wasn't sure if she could forgive Jessica for being so quick to judge, but for her son's sake she was determined to try. She went to buy a nice joint to cook for their meal, plus the makings of Tom's favourite dessert.

In the supermarket Sue noticed that a man ahead of her kept looking behind him. He kept slipping one hand inside his jacket. The other arm was clamped to his chest as if holding something in place. When she reached the spot in which he'd been standing Sue saw the space allocated to the most expensive smoked salmon was empty. The packs would have been thin enough to slip inside a jacket and slippery enough to need holding firmly if they weren't to slip out.

Sue saw a woman come up to the man, exchange a few words and take his trolley to continue shopping. The man walked away slowly, as though not wanting to draw attention to himself, still holding his arm pressed to his side. What should Sue do? Shoplifting pushed up prices for everyone and it didn't seem likely he was stealing through hunger. To her relief she saw a member of staff following the man, meaning she needn't do anything. Sue joined the queue at the till.

As she unloaded her items onto the belt Sue began to doubt the man really was a shoplifter. A moment ago she had been certain, but she hadn't actually seen him take anything and knew from experience things weren't always as they seemed.

What an idiot she'd been! Of course seeing a boot full of toilet rolls just after learning some had been stolen would have made Jessica suspect Sue of taking them. She'd have had to make an immediate decision about whether to act, or allow Sue to drive off with the evidence. As the new girl it had been brave of her to speak up against someone who'd been there for years. She'd jumped to the wrong conclusion, but it was an understandable one.

Sue, apologising to the assistant and those behind her in the queue, threw her shopping back into the trolley and went back to the chilled food aisle. The space for the most expensive smoked salmon was still empty, so she bought the next best. Still pricey, but she thought it worth every penny.

Should she call Tom and ask him to tell Jessica she was forgiven? No. That would make it seem like Sue had held a grudge all this time. Which of course she had…

By Sunday Sue was once again looking forward to meeting the girl she was sure would one day become her daughter-in-law and hopefully someone she'd get on well with. When Tom's car pulled up outside she'd rushed down the path babbling cheerful greetings. She tried to shut up and behave normally. That was suddenly easy when she saw how embarrassed and nervous Jessica looked.

"Hello, Jessica! Lovely to meet you properly this time. Tom you idiot, you didn't tell me Jessica and I briefly met at McIver's!" Well, he had almost forgotten to do so and this seemed the best way to let Jessica know she was remembered, but not with any bad feelings.

"Ooops, sorry," Tom said.

"Well, never mind. Do come in. Oh, are those flowers for me?"

Jessica nodded and handed them over.

"Thank you. Gerberas are my absolute favourite."

"Tom told me."

"Maybe he's not such an idiot after all. He remembers the important things, such as you liking smoked salmon. I bought some especially for today. Come into the kitchen while I put these lovely flowers in water, and I'll tell you what happened in the supermarket."

Sue explained why she thought she'd seen a shoplifter. "When I got back to my car I saw him in one very close by. He was sitting oddly on the passenger seat, with the door open and looked very pale. When I asked if he was OK he said he would be. He explained he'd just had a small operation to remove a growth on his side. His wife collected him from hospital. On the way back she stopped there to buy food. He'd offered to make a start as she parked, but it was a mistake and he'd returned to the car as soon as she found him and that a member of staff had kindly helped him."

"So he was just holding his side because it hurt?"

"Yes, but I hope you can see why I thought the worst?"

At that moment Tom joined them in the kitchen. "Is there something I should know?" he asked.

"No," Sue said at the exact moment Jessica said, "yes."

"Well, which is it?"

Jessica gestured for Sue to go first, so she said, "All you need to know is that you should be pouring the wine."

Jessica laughed. "I had been going to say I think your mum and I will be friends – but now I know we will!"

12. Undeserved Treachery

Shannon answered her phone to hear Liz wailing, "What am I going to do?"

"What's up?" she asked her friend.

"It's Liam. He's been cheating."

"Are you sure?"

"He told me."

"He did what!" Shannon was astounded. This kind of thing happened she knew, but Liam didn't seem the type.

"I wouldn't have known if he hadn't confessed."

"That absolute…"

Liz interrupted with, "He said it was just a mistake and didn't mean anything."

Shannon was furious. "Just wait until I see him! He'll know then what a terrible mistake he's made."

"He says he had to tell me because he couldn't stand the lies."

Shannon thought it might be best if Liz didn't speak to Liam for a while. "He's thoughtless and selfish and not worth you getting upset over. Come round and I'll cheer you up. We'll have pizza and wine, and watch a rubbish film."

"I'd like that," Liz said. "Thanks, mate."

"Bring your toothbrush and stuff."

Shannon ordered an extra large pizza, then put a quilt and pillows in the spare room. She was used to entertaining overnight guests, but the men always shared her bed.

By the time Liz arrived she had wine poured and a pep talk prepared. "He's away a lot, so you'll get custody of the kids. That means you'll get the house and he'll have to pay the bills. I'll give you my lawyer's details – he made sure I did OK out of my divorces."

"Divorce? I don't think he wants that. He feels dreadful about what he's done and wants me to forgive him."

"He feels, he wants. Nothing about how anyone else feels, how you feel, what you want?"

"Not really," Liz admitted.

They drank some wine, ate the pizza when it arrived, then drank more wine.

Liz said, "Actually Liam wasn't just thinking of himself. He arranged for the kids to go to his mum's before he told me, so they wouldn't see me upset. That means he thought about my feelings too, doesn't it?"

"You're thinking of taking him back?"

"There's the kids to consider, Shannon. Us splitting up would really hurt them and… Liam's not perfect I know, but I do love him."

Shannon hugged her. "I'm sorry, I've been a truly rubbish friend."

"No you haven't."

"Yes, I have. I forgot you're nothing like me. I'm superficial when it comes to men. I like them for fun and what I can get out of them, but I've never really cared that much. I see you do. You sure you want him back?"

"Yes – but only if I'm sure he'll never do anything like this again."

"You said he felt awful about what he'd done, and all the lies. He's probably learned his lesson." She refilled their glasses. "I'll help you, and I think I know just what to do."

Shannon's plan was simple. She persuaded Liz to stay with her for a few days, so Liam would see what he'd be missing if he lost his wife. It also gave Liz time to think.

"I let him take me for granted," she told Shannon a few days later. "He could sneak off with another woman because I was always at home looking after the kids. I looked after them, and him, and the house as well as working, and instead of seeing I was tired and helping out he thought I'd got dull and went looking elsewhere for excitement. Well no more! He can do his share, and while he is I'm going to come round and enjoy your company."

Shannon laughed. "Perfect!"

It worked. Liam agreed with all Liz's suggestions and apologised repeatedly, swearing he'd treat her better in future and never cheat again.

"I think he means it," Liz said.

"I'm sure he does," Shannon agreed. She should know, she'd discussed the matter with him the previous day.

"Liz is a wonderful person. You don't deserve her and she doesn't deserve such treachery," Shannon had told him.

"You're totally right," Liam had said, "but you're not the person to tell me. Without you flirting and coming on to me I'd never have had an affair."

"Rubbish. I was very wrong, but I've flirted with plenty of other married men who've ignored me and gone home to their wives. You're a cheat pure and simple and if you ever do it again I'll confess to being your other woman and we'll both lose Liz forever."

13. Exhibition Dance

This feels right. Behind my mask, lost in the crowd of carnival revellers, I'm gloriously free. Alive. The music pours in, controlling my limbs, my muscles, everything that I am. I dance. How could I not? The happiness around me lightens my soul, lifts me up. I abandon myself to it, lost in the joy of the moment.

I know it's wrong. It must be. Everything which brings me joy is wrong, or bad, or childish, or selfish.

"Chris, stop. You're making a spectacle of yourself." I hear Theo as if he were here. He's not. Theo will never join a carnival parade nor watch it pass. He doesn't do anything so silly as joining in with the fun, just for the pleasure of it. He's not spontaneous or uncontrolled. Never swept away in the moment. That's why I'm dancing, being foolish and wild. Like I always do when he's not present to ensure I behave properly. I'm an embarrassment, a cause for shame.

But whose? Not Theo's. He's pushed me away again, to punish me for my failure to conform, to comply. To put on the mask of conventionality and wither away behind it until I become nothing. I'll have to go back, beg forgiveness.

Theo always takes me back when he thinks I've learned my lesson. He thought I had last time. I did too. I really thought I'd become the kind of person Theo says I must be. We were wrong.

Mercifully he can't see me now. Nobody can. All they see is a checkered costume and glittering harlequin mask. And that I'm dancing. I shouldn't, but I dance.

Two men in the most extravagant dresses, with sequins, and feathers, and tassels and beads in their beards, take my hands. They sashay and sway with me. Twirl me around, swoop me back, raise me up just as the music does. I let them. Encourage them. It must be wrong, but it feels right.

No! I cringe as I recognise three faces in the crowd. My ex boss and two former colleagues. I used to believe they liked me. That their smiles when I arrived were because they were cheered by my buoyant greeting, my enthusiasm, my personality. When they laughed and joked I thought it was with me. That they were amused by my quips and exuberance.

Theo explained they laughed at me. An awkward reaction to my embarrassing, unsettling behaviour. He said they were not my friends. "If they were they wouldn't let you behave like a wilful child. They'd make you exercise control."

I'd thought he was right. He must be. But then Theo would be the first to say I often get things wrong, misunderstand, don't know what's good for me.

I'm surrounded by people making a spectacle of themselves, but they're doing no harm. I'm not embarrassed and ashamed for them. I enjoy seeing them happy and having fun. I think my former colleagues do too. Why would they be here if they hated such exhibitions of delight, expressions of happiness, evidence of joy?

For now they're smiling and laughing at the parade, at me as an anonymous part of it. That could change.

I approach, invite them to join me.

"Chris! It really is you," I'm told as they're swept into the parade, become part of the spectacle.

"The real me," I say, though I only just recognise who that is.

"We're glad. We worried something terrible had happened."

"Like what?"

"Theo erasing you."

"He nearly has… If I go back he will. If I don't, I'll have nothing but me. No job, no home."

"Your job is waiting," Lisa, my former boss says.

"Sleep on my sofa until you find something better," offers Julian.

"Or mine," adds Vikki.

These people are my friends. They see the masks I've worn and what's behind them – and dance with me anyway. We're gloriously free. Alive. It feels right.

14. Reasonable Substitutions

As Diane stirred the jug of custard and returned it to the microwave, she couldn't help remembering the time her late mother-in-law had 'caught' her doing just that.

"Oh no, that will never do!" She'd rummaged in the kitchen cupboards and found a saucepan. "Here. Do it properly or there'll be all kinds of trouble."

Diane had grit her teeth, almost regretting the fact the microwaves wouldn't actually cause the other woman any harm. Resisting the urge to bash her mother-in-law with the pan, Diane had transferred the custard and finished it off on the hob.

There had been other instances. She'd been near hysterical at the thought of Diane adding garlic to a dish she was preparing and actually snatched a jar of own label coffee from her hand.

"If you don't have a decent brand, we'll drink tea."

Diane tried to make allowances. Her mother-in-law rarely left the house, other than for food shopping or to stay with their son and Diane, which was probably part of the reason for her being so narrow-minded and stuck in her ways. She occasionally grumbled about the sacrifices she'd made to bring up John, but as far as Diane could see, devotion to her family was just an excuse for never getting a job.

Despite not so subtle hints to the contrary, Diane hadn't neglected her children and husband in order to work as a veterinary nurse. It was a hard and often stressful job. That didn't stop her mother-in-law making comments such as, 'it must be fun playing with cute little kittens' when Diane had to give two-hourly feeds, day and night, to an orphaned litter. Nor did it prevent her expecting homemade food at every meal.

"I did say this week would be difficult and suggest putting your visit back," Diane reminded her.

"Yes, but with less than a fortnight to go. Changing our plans at such short notice would have been impossible," she'd snapped. "We'll just have to make the best of it now. Oh… frozen peas? It would be better to peel some carrots. I'll do it and slice them really thinly, so they cook properly."

How that woman had lived long enough to die of natural causes was a complete mystery. Perhaps she hadn't? Her death was very sudden and the bathroom cabinet was full of different pills which all looked remarkably similar…

"I've been thinking about Dad," John said.

Probably not what she'd been thinking! No, he'd be worried about the old man. Diane was a bit, too. His wife hadn't exactly been a ray of sunshine, but Donald must be lonely and finding it difficult to adjust without her.

"Maybe we should have him here. He can't look after himself," John said.

"There's nothing wrong with him."

"You know what I mean."

She did. He'd been brought up in a different era, when it was more natural to expect women to do all the housework. Besides, his wife was such a stickler that if he'd tried to help she'd just have complained his efforts weren't good enough. As a result he barely knew where the kitchen was and couldn't operate a washing machine. Or even the kettle, judging from the way he frequently suggested tea or coffee, but remained in his chair as Diane sorted it out.

"I know he's a bit difficult, but then I was too when we were first married, remember?"

She did. His mother's fault of course.

John had wanted all his food handmade from scratch, his clothes starched and ironed, proper sheets with hospital corners on the beds and the entire house dusted, scrubbed or polished weekly. And all by her, while he watched football or read the paper.

It hadn't taken long for Diane to explain he had the choice between slightly less exacting standards and a shared workload, or doing it all himself however he thought best.

"Actually the quilt is very comfortable," he'd said. A quick whizz round, by him, with the vacuum cleaner was soon seen as good enough for those weeks his parents weren't visiting and he agreed a takeaway on Friday nights made a nice change.

Donald would be so grateful to her for taking him in that he'd probably adapt even more quickly.

On the way back from collecting him, they went food shopping.

"That's woman's work," Donald said. "John and I will wait in the pub."

Poor man; his wife hadn't even let him have a say in the food they bought!

"I want you to come to make sure we have the things you like," Diane explained.

The concept seemed to confuse him slightly, but once in the store he indicated items he wanted. All his choices were brand names and he turned his nose up at anything readymade or with a whiff of convenience about it. Of course he did, that's what he was used to. It probably wasn't a good idea to suddenly change his diet on top of everything else he had to get used to, so Diane bought what he wanted.

She cooked dinner as John helped his dad unpack and get settled in. Donald ate every scrap of the chicken Chasseur she served, then went and sat in the lounge.

"You have a chat with him while I clear up," Diane suggested to John. "It must seem odd being here on his own and knowing he won't be going home."

She made Donald a mug of Ovaltine to help him sleep and had an early night herself. It wasn't his fault of course, but getting everything ready for Donald and anxiety about how he'd settle in had worn her out. That's probably why she overslept despite his snoring.

John had already left for work when she got up. His company were in the middle of an important project, so Diane had taken the Friday off to keep Donald company. There was no sign of him yet, so she had her own breakfast and cleared up from the night before. John and Donald must have found a lot to talk about as they'd forgotten to do it. Even the mug from Donald's milky drink had been left in the lounge.

She loaded the dishwasher, emptied the bins and then decided that as it was her day off she'd sit in the sun and read. Three chapters later she went in to make herself a coffee. It was strange to be in the house on her own with nothing much to do.

Donald! Of course, that's why she wasn't at work. She glanced at the clock. It was almost lunchtime. Why wasn't he up yet? Or had he come down, been unable to find her and thought he'd been abandoned? No, he'd have seen the kitchen door open and looked out, surely? Was he ill? Or worse… he'd been snoring loudly last night, but now there was silence.

Diane raced upstairs and into his room.

"At last!" he said. "Where's my coffee?"

When they'd stayed before, his wife had always got up early and, loudly, made their coffee. Diane wasn't about to dictate to a grown man what time he should get up.

"Everything you need is down in the kitchen. You just go and help yourself whenever you like," she told him.

She was unloading the dishwasher when he eventually appeared.

"I hope you haven't put my mug in that contraption. It isn't hygienic."

Diane explained that, as it used a higher temperature, it was far more hygienic than washing by hand, but he didn't seem to be listening.

"What's that?" He gestured to the carton of semi-skimmed milk she'd put on the table for him.

"For your cereal, if you want some?"

"Cereals! No, bacon and eggs. That's a proper breakfast."

It was gone one by then and his wife had always served lunch at twelve thirty exactly, plus of course he hadn't eaten all morning. He must be hungry and bacon would be quicker to do than the salad lunch she'd planned.

"Coming right up!"

The rest of the day was a little strained. Poor Donald seemed disorientated and at times apparently confused her with his late wife. She did her best to soothe him, but couldn't get him to try out their cordless kettle or even the TV remote, though he was happy enough to watch the snooker and drink coffee all afternoon.

Diane was pleased to see John when he came home, though puzzled that he'd brought a pint of full fat milk. They never used it.

"For Dad," he explained. "He says he can't drink the green label stuff."

"He seemed happy with it in his Ovaltine last night and in all the coffees I've made him today."

John shrugged. "He texted to ask me to bring some on my way home."

"Texted! He uses a mobile phone, but won't touch the kettle?"

"I suppose he's used to Mum doing it."

"You're right and that's the milk he's used to."

Donald was horrified at her suggestion she 'bung a couple of jacket potatoes in the microwave' to go with their evening meal, so she'd peeled and mashed them. He'd been suspicious of the own label sausages, so she'd cooked chops instead, after hastily defrosting them in the microwave once he was back in the lounge.

"So, do you want to wash or dry?" she said brightly as she collected up the plates.

"Thought you had a machine for that?"

She smiled. He was coming round to her way of thinking already.

That evening he cheerfully assured Diane he could taste the difference in his Ovaltine. Odd as she'd forgotten about his bottle and used to same semi-skimmed milk she and John drank.

John easily slept through his father's snoring, but Diane couldn't. She tried earplugs, but they were uncomfortable and didn't help much. Thankfully her doctor was sympathetic and prescribed sleeping tablets.

"They're very effective, but only a short term solution," she said.

The doctor was right. Just one pill and Diane was assured of eight hours uninterrupted sleep. She felt much better from the very first morning and much more able to cope with her father-in-law's ingrained habits and what he believed to be his preferences.

When their daughter came on Saturday, Diane offered to make her favourite spag Bol.

"I can't eat that foreign muck," Donald said.

Before Diane could snap that her cooking wasn't 'muck' and point out he'd wolfed down her chicken Chasseur on Thursday without complaint, she was interrupted.

"It's just spaghetti, Grandad. You like that."

"Oh. Spaghetti? Why didn't you say?"

"Spag Bol, garlic bread and green salad coming right up," Diane said.

"Garlic?" Donald queried, as though she'd suggested rat poison.

"Yes, the stuff I put five cloves of in the chicken Chassuer," Diane said, but only in her head. Out loud she said, "Would you rather not have any in yours?" She had an idea.

She made one big batch of garlicky sauce, then spooned some into another pan for Donald, adding a squirt of own label tomato sauce so it looked slightly different. She took a couple of slices of readymade garlic bread out the oven when it was still pale and sprinkled on extra parsley and let him think she'd made him herb bread from scratch. He ate the lot.

Diane started substituting all kinds of things. She kept the bottle the full-fat milk came in, rinsing and refilling it from the large carton of semi-skimmed. She gave him sweeteners in his coffee instead of sugar and filled the shaker with rock salt instead of ground so none came out when Donald shook it over his food. A couple of times she even dug her fingernails into a green bean and pretended to have shelled fresh peas instead of cooking frozen ones. It was a silly game really, but it amused her and helped hide her growing irritation with her father-in-law.

Only gradually did the truth about Donald dawn on her. He wasn't just used to certain types of food, he was actually very difficult to please unless he believed they'd bought the best of everything and Diane had spent a long time preparing complicated recipes from scratch. He wasn't wary of modern appliances, just too idle to help out around the house. Slowly Diane began to see that out of her in-laws, she'd given her sympathy to the wrong one.

The third most irritating thing about Donald was that the few times he realised she'd made a change, he accused her of trying to cause him some kind of harm. That was annoying when was doing quite the opposite; his doctor had advised cutting down fat and salt to help his blood pressure.

Second worst was that John was starting to follow his father's example and expect Diane to run around after him, just as his mother once had. On the few occasions he made the coffee she noticed the level of milk had only dropped in the bottle which supposedly held full fat. After eating two helpings of the bought fruit pie she'd served to follow the roast dinner she'd spent all morning cooking he said, "It's not as good as homemade."

It occurred to Diane that she could sprinkle flour on the kitchen work tops to mimic home baking. She'd have to clear up afterwards though and need to continue it along with all her other little ruses. Why should she have to do that, just to get a bit of peace in her own home?

The very worst though was her father-in-law's reaction when she pointed out that she didn't have time for her job and to look after the pair of them, especially when one required almost constant attention.

Donald had the answer. "You will once you give up playing with other people's animals. There's my pension and there will be money when the house is sold, so you can stay at home."

"Isn't that generous of Dad?" John said later that night. "Of course you'll have to be careful not to upset him again. He says you're sometimes a bit sharp with him and…"

Diane stopped listening and began planning one final substitution. All she had to do was swap the heart tablets Donald took four times a day and the painkillers he gulped whenever she hinted he operate the vacuum cleaner, with her sleeping tablets. After all, the doctor had said they were only a temporary solution. Once Donald had swallowed enough, she wouldn't need them any more.

15. My Version Of Reality

Sean glanced at his watch and considered what to do. If he walked straight to the clocktower he'd be exactly on time to meet Maria at twelve as he'd arranged. That would please her and should therefore make her want to please him. On the other hand she'd been getting a bit of her old confidence back lately and he didn't like that.

A sign offering a free florentine with every cappuccino in Luigi's cafe convinced Sean not to take the risk. The fancy little cookies were delicious and usually cost more than the cappuccino, which was his favourite type of coffee. He'd meet Maria at twelve-thirty claiming that was the time they'd agreed. After enjoying his snack he could go without lunch until she said she was starving, which by his calculations would be just when he'd 'suddenly remember' the appointment at the bank. He'd gain her gratitude by agreeing to eat soon, despite him having told her to have breakfast before going out. He'd said the opposite of course, but knew she'd doubt herself. That insecurity would make her reluctant to question the banking arrangements which he'd reassure her, and the branch manager, they'd already been through and agreed. If she did feel brave enough to insist on reading the forms before signing, her hunger would ensure she skimmed through quickly so they could go to eat. He'd take her to her favourite restaurant, Quattro, and then for a boat trip down the river, just as he'd promised, to convince her everything was OK.

Sean strode up to Luigi's and walked straight into the reinforced glass door. That hurt his forehead and pride in equal measure.

"Are you OK?" asked a waiter, after unlocking the door.

"No! Why wasn't this open?"

"It's only five to twelve."

"You open at eleven."

The waiter shook his head and indicated the sign with the opening times, which did indeed say twelve. "Perhaps you're thinking of somewhere else?"

"I must be..." But surely he'd had coffee in there much earlier in the day on several occasions quite recently. It was a horrible feeling to doubt himself like that and he'd like to have been able to confirm his memory hadn't let him down. Unfortunately he couldn't ask Maria as he'd not been there with her recently. On their one and only joint visit she'd spoken in Italian to the members of staff in a very familiar manner. No way was he going to put up with her having a conversation he couldn't understand.

"What can I get you?" the waiter asked.

"Cappuccino and a florentine."

"We have a special offer on. If you have a latte instead, the florentine is free."

"But the sign says..." Only when he turned to point it out, he saw it did indeed say latte, not cappuccino.

"Wishful thinking, maybe?" the waiter said.

No wonder Maria had been so easy to convince that what she thought she remembered as his promises, had really been wishful thinking on her part. It seemed that could happen for real.

"Right. Well, I'll have what's on the offer then."

"Coming right up!"

A few minutes later the waiter reappeared. "OK, we're officially open now, so I can take your order. What can I get you?"

What was going on? He'd definitely already ordered. Was the waiter messing with him because he'd been abrupt after walking into the door he was still almost sure should already have been open? Other customers were coming in now, so the bloke wouldn't be able to get away with anything else like that. Sean knew how important it was to avoid witnesses if you intended to slightly misinterpret reality.

"I'd like the coffee and cake offer advertised in the window, please," he said politely, but quite loudly. He wasn't going to be told he'd ordered the wrong thing and would therefore have to pay full price.

Sean enjoyed his coffee, and the florentine was exceptional. There wasn't, as he'd thought possible, any problem over the offer. He was only charged the usual price for a latte, or a cappuccino come to that.

Maria wasn't waiting at the clock tower when he arrived. Had something happened to her? She was never late, as she knew how he hated to be kept waiting, so should have been there for over thirty minutes. Just as he was thinking of calling her, she appeared on the other side of the square. She wasn't even hurrying!

"What's up, love?" she asked when she finally put an end to his wait.

"You're late!" he said.

"Oh! I'm sorry, Sean. I'm glad it's just that though, you looked as though something was really wrong."

"It is. You know I hate hanging round looking a fool because you've not shown up on time."

"Yes, of course. It's not a nice feeling, but look," she pointed to the clock tower. "Eleven forty-five. We're both early."

"That's wrong." He showed his watch as proof.

"Oh, I must have made a mistake… No, for once it seems I'm right." She showed him her watch, which indicated the same time as the clocktower.

Sean pulled out his phone and snatched Maria's from her pocket, leaving her to pick up the scrap of paper which fluttered to the ground. Both showed eleven forty-six.

"Your watch is fast, that's all," Maria soothed.

That would explain the cafe not being open. The waiter had said it was almost twelve, but he'd been an idiot. There was the sign though…

"Are you OK, Sean?" She placed a gentle hand in his forehead.

"I'm fine." He wasn't going to think about this any more, it was too confusing.

"Not eaten something which has disagreed with you?"

"I said I'm fine!" Although her repeatedly asking was making him feel a little under the weather. He must remember that technique as it was a brilliant way to undermine someone's happiness and energy, whilst seeming kind and concerned.

"Oh good, I'm looking forward to the boat trip."

"We're doing that this afternoon."

"Twelve thirty, yes. That's why you said to make sure I have a good breakfast and be here by twelve."

Just as Sean was getting worried he was losing his hold over her she frowned, then in a quieter voice added,"I'm sure you did."

Maria looked uncomfortable and fumbled with the scrap of paper she'd picked up. That was better.

Suddenly her face cleared and she smiled, which wasn't so good. "Oh! You ate at Luigi's. That's all right then. For a minute I thought I'd got things wrong again."

What had he been thinking by keeping that receipt? He usually disposed of any evidence which could prove anyone but him in the right. It must have been because he'd been worried about getting overcharged. Sean was really starting to hate that waiter – he'd have to find a way to make him pay.

Sean had planned to use the boat trip to show off his recently researched knowledge of the places they'd pass, impressing Maria with his superior intelligence, but could hardly keep his eyes open. Fortunately she was too entranced to pay him much attention, other than occasionally pointing out something which caught her interest.

Afterwards Maria wanted to wait to see the boat set off with the next lot of passengers so she could take a photograph. He was more than happy to go along with that, as the delay would fit in well with his plan of almost missing the appointment at the bank, so business would be conducted as quickly as possible. It would also allow him to slip into the nearby newsagent and grab a snack. That florentine hadn't kept hunger away as long as he'd hoped and it seemed they weren't going to Quattro after all. He was starting to get confused over which were things he'd actually said and which were things he'd planned to tell maria he'd said.

"Sean?"

"Hmm?"

"You'll need to stand here to be in the photo."

He recognised the tone of voice, despite it usually being him who talked to her as though she needed guidance to achieve the simplest things. Hoping the bank manager would offer tea and biscuits, Sean tried to look as self assured as usual in a series of selfies.

"Do you fancy a snack?" he asked afterwards.

"I don't want to spoil my appetite before we get to Quattro."

"Quattro?" So he had booked it.

"You did remember to book? Our reward for sorting out the bank stuff, you said."

"I did, yes, absolutely." Had he really told her about going to the bank? Of course he had in a general way, to prepare the ground for taking sole control of their joint finances, but he didn't think he'd mentioned that day's appointment. He'd considered it, thinking it would be better not for the bank manager to think he'd sprung it on her. He really must get a grip – liars can't afford to have bad memories.

"We'd better get going. We don't want to be late."

She might not, but he most definitely did. How could he delay things? He couldn't sit on a bench and take a snooze, however tempting that idea was. "Let's go this way. I think it's shorter." He hated having to speak with uncertainty, but as going in the direction he'd indicated would add several minutes to the journey, he had no option.

Maria played right into his hands by turning left instead of right at the end of the alley. He let her go quite a distance by pointing out her mistake. "I didn't think it was right, but you seemed so sure."

"Oh dear, I am sorry," she said, sounding nicely flustered. "Do you think they'll still see us? Or maybe it would be better if they don't, as I don't seem to be with it today."

"Don't worry," Sean soothed. "You just leave everything to me."

"Thanks, Sean. I'm so glad I have you to rely on. I'd get myself into an awful mess otherwise." She'd reached the first bank in the row of three, which was where they both had separate accounts, but walked past. After some careful persuasion on his part they'd agreed on a completely new account in a completely new bank.

Maria pushed open the door of the second bank. Sean was just about to say she'd made a mistake, when a member of staff approached them. "Mr Turner, Miss Romano?"

"That's us. Sorry we're late."

"These things happen, but unfortunately I have another appointment in twenty minutes."

"I'm sure we can get through things quickly," Sean said. Obviously this was the right bank. They wouldn't be expected otherwise. The appointment right after theirs was a stroke of luck. He just had to focus on the positives, get the paperwork signed and then work out what was going on with his head.

The bank manager ushered them into his office, invited them to take a seat and took away their ID to be photocopied.

"Is your head troubling you?" Maria asked with concern.

"My head?"

She gently touched his forehead as she'd done earlier that day. "You've got a bruise. I wondered if you'd banged it somewhere."

Of course! He'd walked into the door at Luigi's. It must have affected his memory. He couldn't admit that now though. If he did, Maria might want to postpone the paperwork and take him to hospital, and he couldn't wait for the money to be put into his name.

Or rather the unpleasant individual who'd seemed so friendly when Sean had taken out the loan wouldn't wait. He was using that money to convince Maria they were financial equals. The investment should have paid off two weeks ago, but he'd made a mistake in softening Maria up. His kindness to her had made her brave enough to start asking questions and he'd had to unsettle her all over again to be sure she'd sign without reading everything first. His creditor was unsympathetic and declared time was up. Honestly, even without the bang on the head it wasn't surprising he was losing his touch with all the stress he'd been under lately.

"Mr Turner?" the bank manager said.

"Yes?" Oh, he was offering a pen. "Thank you." He wrote his name next to Maria's on page after page of documents. All the while assuring the bank manager they understood perfectly what they were agreeing to.

Once they were out of the bank, Maria again asked him if he was OK.

"I feel much better, just a little tired," he told her honestly.

"Let's go into Luigi's and have a coffee, shall we?" she said. "That will revive you."

He regretted agreeing to that as soon as she started chattering away in Italian to the idiot waiter. "What are you saying?" he demanded.

"Just talking about gaslighting."

"What?"

"You know, the way you cut me off from my friends and family so there is no one to tell me that your version of reality isn't true."

"But I..." If she'd guessed, why had she signed the paperwork?

"Of course trying to keep me away from my family means you don't know them either. This is my cousin Alessandro."

Sean sneered. "You're always talking about your family as though they're something special, but he's just a waiter."

"There's absolutely nothing wrong with being a waiter. Several of my family work here, as the café is owned by my uncle. Not Alessandro though. He works in a bank. Not the one where you tried to get your hands on my money."

"Tried to...?"

"You're really not with it today, are you, Sean? Remember your watch is fast?"

He nodded.

"Odd then that we were late for the bank appointment."

"It was the wrong bank!"

"Wrong for you, yes. You've just signed everything over to me."

As he thought of the angry loan shark he'd never be able to pay, Sean slumped in his seat.

"I wish you hadn't hit him with the door," Maria said, in Italian. "There could be witnesses."

"Don't worry, Maria Bella, no witnesses and no evidence now I've destroyed the altered offer poster and list of opening times. Besides, Sean here brought all this on himself. The arrogant fool banged his own head, and by gaslighting you, he showed you how to do the same to him."

16. A Job To Hide

Alan heard his mates laughing outside Woolworths from halfway down the street. He didn't wonder what the joke was as there wouldn't be one; they only seemed to be amused by the misfortune of others. That's unless it was at one of those bubble cars and then the laughter would be to cover their envy. None of the gang was ever likely to be able to buy a decent pair of the new cuban heeled boots, let alone a car. For the first time Alan wondered why he still hung around with lads who considered themselves cooler than The Beatles, but his mum called a bunch of long haired yobs.

At school it was because Shane had said, "Are you with us, or against us?" The gang leader made it clear neutrality wasn't an option. Back then it had been quite a big group and Alan stayed safely on the edges – neither being bullied, nor picking on others. It was harder to avoid attention now there were fewer of them. Some had managed to get jobs, others were in youth offending institutions.

"Losers the lot of them," was Shane's opinion. The criminals were fools for getting caught, and those with jobs stupid for being caught in the system.

Maybe he was right, but Shane, Alan, and the rest weren't exactly winners. They never would be and there seemed little point even hoping things would be different.

"Heard about that idiot Jacob?" Shane asked when Alan reached him.

Alan shook his head. Jacob had gradually spent less time with the gang and dropped out completely about a month ago. Like Alan, Jacob always kept out of trouble as much as he could. Like the whole gang, he'd once stolen a record for Shane, to prove his loyalty. Jacob was so nervous he'd grabbed one by The Temptations and was demoted to lookout after that. Surely he hadn't done anything bad enough to get arrested for?

"Only got himself a job in the Bluebird Café," one of gang sneered.

"What a mug! Menial work for a pittance, all the time sucking up to the saddos who've got nothing better to do than drink tea in that dump. Pathetic."

Although Shane made it sound like a terrible fate, Alan thought the work might be a welcome change from hanging around on cold street corners, drinking cheap beer and breathing in smoke from the others. Saying 'no problem, I'll get that right away' might be nicer than calling out insults to passing strangers, especially if he got paid for it.

He'd seen the café. It wasn't modern, loud or fashionable like the burger place. Not somewhere the gang would go if they could afford to eat out, but Alan quite liked the idea of a chat over a piece of cake. It would be a bit like talking to Mum at teatime had been, when he was still at school and before she worked night shifts.

Something of that must have shown on his face, because Shane prodded him in the chest. "What's on your mind, Mr Squeaky Clean? Want to go over and congratulate him, do you?"

"Nah. Be pointless." He couldn't imagine Shane really would say anything positive and none of them had any of their dole money left.

"I reckon we should," Shane surprised him by saying. "Come on lads. Let's have a nice cup of tea with our old friend."

Alan, feeling slightly worried, went along with them.

The gang barged in, noisily dragging chairs about so they could sit together. The customers, except for a toddler who'd started to whimper, fell silent.

Jacob, with an apron round his waist, notebook in hand and expression which showed he'd rather be somewhere else, approached. "What do you lot want?"

"I think you mean, 'What would you like, sir?' We'll have coffee all round and lots of cakes on those fancy stand things." Shane gestured at two elderly ladies who'd stopped enjoying their meal to stare in alarm at the gang. "And make it snappy."

Jacob took a deep breath. "Can you pay for it?" His voice came out in a squeak.

"We ain't going to. It'll be on the house, seeing we're mates of yours."

"I can't do that," Jacob managed to reply.

"Some mate you are! We've always stuck up for you and kept quiet about your shoplifting."

Alan, seeing the desperation on his former friend's face, wished he'd tried to stop the gang going to the Bluebird. Maybe Shane thought he was being tough or funny or something, but all he was doing was risking Jacob's job. That's not what a real mate would do.

"Let's get out of here, Shane," Alan said. "I don't want to hang around with this loser." He stood up, shoving his chair away so hard it fell over, and strode towards the door. "He's welcome to his rubbish job, old ladies and crying babies. We've got better things to do."

Alan's heart was hammering by the time he got outside. Whether he saw the reason behind them or not, Jacob might hate Alan for those insults, but he was more worried about Shane's reaction. The gang had followed Alan out. Shane was the last to leave and didn't look happy.

"Come on then, Einstein, what's your big idea?"

Alan kept walking, trying to think of something. Anything.

"We could go over the park." They'd frighten away the mums with little kids and tangle up the swings so they'd be out of action until a man from the council sorted them out, but shouldn't be able to do any real harm.

"Park's about right for a mummy's boy like you," Shane snarled, but headed in that direction anyway.

Once he was sure the gang were going to keep away from the café, Alan left them, intending to go back to the flat. Mum would be asleep, so he couldn't play music, but it wouldn't be any more boring than watching Shane spit at pigeons.

On his way home, Alan saw an old lady struggling to lift her tartan shopping trolley up the steps to her front door. She was dressed so brightly, and her difficulty so clear, she was totally unmissable. Shane would have laughed or shouted insults. Alan would have been helpless to stop him, but Shane wasn't there. Alan hopped over the gate and shifted the trolley for the woman. Then he remembered how old people often found the gang members intimidating and mumbled, "I didn't mean to startle you. It just looked like that was heavy."

"It was a different bus driver," the woman said as if that explained something. "He didn't drop me off on the corner, so I had to walk all the way from the stop up by Queen Street. I could do with a cup of tea, I can tell you."

She'd let herself in as she spoke, leaving Alan to follow with the shopping trolley.

"As you're here, be a dear and open the new jar of marmalade, would you?"

By the time Alan found it, loosened the top and put it in the cupboard, the lady had filled the kettle and set out two cups and two small plates.

"Fetch the cake tin, would you?" She gestured to the pantry.

Alan spotted a big cream tin, which he placed on the kitchen table.

"You'll have a slice."

"I…"

"I'll never eat it all before it goes stale and I hate to waste good food. Put everything on a tray and bring it into the front room."

Just as with Shane, the lady didn't give him much option but to go along with her wishes. Alan didn't mind sitting on her lumpy settee; it was more comfortable than the brick walls which were his usual seat and, as she'd put a match to the fire, the room was warming up. The cake was lovely.

The old lady asked him his name and told him she was Mrs Swift. She chattered away about everything from the weather being good for the garden to her amazement they were thinking of sending a man to the moon. It was sort of nice in a way. She was very positive and asked his opinion on things she'd read about in the newspaper. That reminded him of how Mum used to talk to him. Now he hardly saw her and when he did she was tired.

"Have you got a job?" the old lady asked.

Alan shook his head. He'd tried to get one after school, so Mum didn't need to do so many hours, but with the factory where most people in the town had worked closing down it was hopeless.

"You'd like one though?"

"There's not much about and everyone wants qualifications and references and that."

"There are things you could do for me; cutting the grass, cleaning windows and bringing in coal. I don't have much money, but I could give you a few shillings "

Alan had already guessed Mrs Swift wasn't rich. She didn't have a phone or a TV that he'd seen. Her place was crammed with nicknacks and ornaments. For all Alan knew they could be valuable, but most looked like holiday souvenirs. Still, even a bit more money would be good and it was something to do.

"Yeah, all right then."

"I like a routine and something to look forward to. Shall we say you'll be here at nine o'clock every Tuesday?"

Alan often wasn't up by nine, but didn't like to say so. "OK."

Hanging about in the street with the gang felt even more boring than usual after meeting Mrs Swift. They were so negative about everything and wanted everyone as unhappy as they were. It was working; their attitude dragged him down.

On the Tuesday morning, Alan got up earlier than he had for months. Mum came in just as he was making toast, so he did her some. She looked so pleased, and so tired, that once she'd eaten it he told her to go off to bed and that he'd wash up.

"You're a good lad," she said.

Alan remembered that even after thinking Jacob's job of making tea and sandwiches in the warm sounded better than hanging about with Shane, he hadn't thought of doing that for his mum. He hadn't been a good son to her, but he'd try to be from now on.

At Mrs Swift's he cut the grass and raked up some leaves, cleared a blocked gutter and replaced a lightbulb. When Alan left, with a very small number of shillings, he was was shocked to realise he'd been there for three hours. It was good to feel useful and she'd kept praising him for being so kind and doing a good job. He couldn't remember the last time anyone had been impressed with him and it had happened twice in one day.

Alan was grinning when he met up with the others.

"Where you been?" Shane demanded.

Alan had no intention of telling them. Fortunately, from his cheerful expression someone guessed he'd been with a woman.

"Can't deny it," he said. He grinned again when the gang showed him something like respect. If only they knew!

Over the next few weeks Alan made breakfast for his mum every Tuesday morning and on other days if he got up early enough. He washed up afterwards too. Both Mum and Mrs Swift continued to praise him, sometimes for qualities he didn't have. Alan found he wanted their words to be true, so spent less time with the gang and more at home, and with Mrs Swift.

"I can't pay you any more, lad, but I could give you your lunch."

Alan regularly went shopping with Mrs Swift, so he could help carry the extra ingredients. On their return she showed him how to prepare meals, encouraging him to have a try. Soon Alan was contributing his shillings so two or three times a week they could make extra large cottage pies, lamb hotpots and chicken stew and Alan could take a portion home for his mum. Sometimes he even remembered to clear up a bit before going to bed in the evenings, so the flat was nearly as tidy when she came in from work as it had been when she left.

"You don't know what a difference it makes, having you help out like this," she said.

Alan was beginning to. She was much less tired now, the difference being greater than could be accounted for by the amount of housework he did. Doing everything herself had been getting her down, just as hanging out with Shane's gang had depressed Alan. He was sure that even though Mrs Swift had been cheerful since their first meeting, she too enjoyed his company. He should be sure, as she kept saying that she'd miss him once he had a proper job. She sounded so confident that he'd get one, Alan wondered if it might be worth trying again.

Visiting Mrs Swift more often had only one downside; it increased his chances of being seen there. Eventually Shane spotted Alan carrying shopping into her house. He'd fetched the gang and waited.

"What you up to?" Shane demanded when Alan emerged.

Alan wanted to say it was none of Shane's business, but couldn't risk him deciding to torment Mrs Swift as revenge for Alan standing up to him in front of the others. He crossed the road and joined the group as though that's what he'd been on his way to do.

"Having a look round, seeing if there was anything worth nicking."

"Is there?" Shane asked.

Fortunately he could tell the truth there. "Nah, a load of rubbish."

"Just like you then."

As the gang laughed, Alan realised it wasn't true. He didn't have any qualifications because they'd convinced him it wasn't worth bothering. That, and their attitude to work rubbing off on him, meant he'd not stood a chance of getting the few jobs he'd applied for. Hanging around with them instead of doing something useful made him feel ever more miserable. At last he'd broken free of that vicious circle.

"If I'm rubbish, you won't want me hanging around." He walked away and didn't look back.

Alan walked in a big loop and, after checking the gang had moved on, returned to Mrs Swift's house. On his way back in, he watered her pot of geraniums, the job he'd gone out to do thirty minutes previously. He explained the reason for his absence and then found himself telling her everything.

"I think you're ready," she announced.

"For what?" Alan asked.

"A job."

"Yeah, I should try." He would too.

"There's a vacancy in the Bluebird Café. How would you feel about working there?"

"I dunno." He'd like that, but didn't think the owner would want him.

"It's a good place to start. I was a waitress there myself once and Well, that's a long and an old story. I think it would suit you."

"Yeah, might do."

"I'll give you a reference. I can say you're punctual, you can cook simple meals, and that you're honest and resourceful, because that's all true, isn't it?"

"Yeah… I suppose it is."

At the café, Jacob gave him an application form. "I'll put in a good word for you," he promised.

"Thanks. If I get it, I'll work hard and not let you down, you'll see."

"Actually I won't." Jacob explained he'd got a new job in the local hotel. "It's doing the same kind of work to start, but I'll get training and the chance to work myself up. The person who I took over from here did the same and maybe you could too."

"If I get this job. All I've got is one reference."

It was a really good one though. Mrs Swift seemed to know exactly what to say. The person she described did sound like Alan, but a version of Alan who'd be a good choice to work in a café.

"It's easy enough once you know how and I've written lots of these," she said, when Alan expressed his gratitude.

Alan got Mum to cut his hair and he dressed in his smartest clothes for the interview. At first he was nervous, but he followed Mum and Mrs Swift's advice to tell the truth.

"What have you done since leaving school?"

Alan admitted that he'd not done much except get into a bit of minor trouble to start with, but lately he'd been helping an old lady.

"Mrs Swift?"

"Yeah."

"And did she teach you to make a cottage pie as good as the one Jacob does?"

"She taught him?"

"Yes. And me, and lots of other people in between."

Not long after getting over that surprise, Alan was shaking hands with the boss and saying he looked forward to starting work on the following Monday.

Mum would still be asleep, so Alan went straight to Mrs Swift's house to share the good news. He saw her, wearing an orange hat and purple coat, struggling to lift the tartan shopping trolley up the steps to her front door. Before Alan reached her, a lad hopped over the gate and ran up the path behind her. He wasn't one of the gang members, but even so Alan was concerned he might be up to no good and sped up. Then he saw the lad shift the shopping trolley and heard Mrs Swift saying how far away the bus stop was and that she was in need of a cup of tea.

Alan turned away. He would thank Mrs Swift for helping him get the job, but he'd come back another time to do that. If he didn't interrupt her now he wouldn't need to apologise for no longer having so much free time to come and help her, as his replacement would already be in place. He wondered how long it would be before, like dominoes, that boy took his job in the café and Alan took Jacob's job in the hotel.

Once Alan was earning, his mum cut her hours and returned to day shifts. Soon she was the happy, optimistic woman he remembered. By the time she married his step-dad, Alan had moved from working in the Bluebird to the hotel, where he was able to live in, so that worked out perfectly. He did indeed receive training there, but didn't work his way up to Maitre 'd as Jacob eventually did. Instead he'd returned to the Bluebird Café, first as assistant manager, then manager, finally buying the place from his former boss. Every year, on his holiday, Alan bought Mrs Swift one of those china nicknacks she seemed so fond of.

Now Mrs Swift is long gone, though not forgotten. Alan has himself retired, but still maintains an interest in the Bluebird Café. He and his wife often have lunch there. They did that today, then walked home.

Alan's bringing in his wheelie bin, but apparently hasn't noticed a bright turquoise plastic bag jammed up in one of the wheels, and he's struggling to move it.

A girl in fashionably ripped jeans, bleached blonde hair and a nose stud, hops over the wall and pulls it free for him. "Sorry, didn't mean to startle you, but I saw this was giving you trouble." She holds up the bag.

"Blown by the wind I expect," Alan says. "Proper dries you out this weather does, I need a cup of tea I can tell you."

Alan talks about the weather as he opens the side gate and walks round to the back of the house, leaving the girl to follow with the bin. He calls out to his wife that they have a visitor. She'd baked a lovely cake the day before. They don't really need help eating it, but they'll offer the girl a slice anyway.

17. Fido The Assistance Dog

Three in the morning it was, when I spotted two girls walking towards me. Well, I say walking; they were wearing the kind of shoes which are designed for sitting down and looking pretty in, and they'd had more than a few drinks. They were talking in that way which seems quiet to those who've been drinking, but really isn't.

"There'sh a man coming."

"Wash he doing?"

"Dunno."

Hiding in the bushes is what I was doing. Doesn't sound too good, does it? I don't have a daughter, but if I did I know I wouldn't want her stumbling in from a night out, reporting she'd spotted a man hiding in the bushes.

"Come on, boy, hurry up," I stage whispered. It did the trick.

"He'sh walking hish dog."

"Ooooh. Nice lickle doggy."

If they remembered the incident at all, which seemed unlikely, they'd probably have been able to describe my totally imaginary 'nice little doggie'. I was soon on my way home, hoping they too would soon be safely tucked up in their beds and that their parents weren't waiting too anxiously.

That awkward incident made me feel lonely. There's no one who waits at home for me, anxiously or otherwise. No one to go out with at night either. In my line of work that isn't advisable and the people I meet when 'on duty' as it were, usually aren't the sort I want to be friends with away from work.

A dog though, that would be different. He'd be company, would help people feel less nervous when they saw me out and about, and maybe I could even teach it to be useful. Even so, it didn't immediately occur to me to get one myself.

Because of the unsociable hours I work, I end up watching daytime TV now and then. The next day there was a programme on about dogs especially trained to help sick or disabled people. Absolutely incredible what they could do. Some alerted owners if they were going to have an epileptic fit or their blood sugar was dropping dangerously low. I think everyone knows about guide dogs for the blind, but they have them for deaf people too. These let their owners know if the phone or alarm is ringing and use a code to say who is at the door if the bell goes. Then there are those which pick up things like dropped phones for disabled people, take the wallet from their bag and put it on a shop counter or operate the washing machine. Honestly and truly they do!

I'm lucky enough not to need anything like that. Perhaps I did vaguely wonder what a dog could do for me, but not seriously. Maybe it was just the programme making me more aware of them, but over the next few days it seemed that dogs, or at least mentions of them, were everywhere.

A family playing ball in the park with theirs, 'beware of the dog' signs on gates, or 'lost dog' posters on lamp posts. A dog barking in the night disturbed the peace, although not as much as the people leaning out of nearby houses and yelling at it to shut up did. Police and guard dogs patrolling, leaflets about the local rescue place and the dogs in need of homes.

I set off down there to get one. It wasn't quite as quick or simple as I'd imagined. There were questions to answer and someone had to come and inspect my place to make sure it was suitable. I wasn't too worried; it's not a big place but there's not much in it, so plenty of room for a dog.

The wait gave me an opportunity to spend time with lots of the dogs awaiting new homes and I made the most of that, befriending as many as possible as I made my choice. One of the volunteers, Ruth I think her name was, showed me round and introduced me to to animals.

"They know if you're a dog person or not and respond accordingly," Ruth said.

Happily most of the dogs seemed to take to me. One of the options was a three legged terrier.

"He's still a lively little thing," Ruth said. "Of course his injury will make it harder to home him."

It didn't worry me too much. We're none of us perfect are we? Still, it seemed sensible not to make a snap decision.

Next one along was a huge Afghan hound.

"Lovely, isn't she?"

I agreed.

"She'd need lots of exercise."

"That's no problem. I could take her on a good long run every night."

"Best keep her on the lead though as she doesn't always come back when called."

I made a mental note of that and reluctantly decided the gorgeous and striking looking creature wasn't suitable for me.

There was one tiny little thing which seemed terrified of me.

"Sadly she doesn't like men and we suspect it's because she's been badly treated."

I left her alone. We'd be no help to each other.

Next was a Rottweiler. I was assured he was gentle and placid, and that seemed to be the case. He rolled over for his tummy to be scratched and drooled all over me. He looked ferocious when on his feet though. Seeing me with him wouldn't reassure anyone late at night.

My mind kept going back to the three legged terrier. I was tempted, but the very fact he was so memorable dissuaded me. An animal with so much character was bound to find a home somewhere.

Then I spotted Fido.

Ruth sounded almost apologetic the creature had such an unimaginative name, but it suited him perfectly. Fido just looked like a little brown dog. Quite cute but not outstanding in any way. A reasonable amount of hair, floppy ears and waggy tail. Could be a description of any dog, but it's not. It's a description of the one I wanted to be mine.

I explained to the people at the rescue place that I wanted to take Fido to work with me and to train him to be useful. Obviously I was pretty vague about how he could help and the details about what I actually do were none existent, but they still seemed keen on the idea. After I'd spent some time getting to know the dog and they'd inspected my home, they were satisfied. So was I. Fido is an absolutely perfect companion.

There's no worries about him intimidating anyone for a start. If people see me out with him anywhere, anytime, they don't have to stop and wonder what I'm doing as clearly I'm walking my dog. In that way he reduces the attention people pay to me, but he does draw some himself. People often want to stroke him and that's fine with me. He can take any amount of fussing and although they barely glance up at me it makes them see me as a nice, harmless individual.

Fido was already housetrained and would sit and stay when I told him, but I was pretty sure he was capable of a lot more than that.

I threw sticks for him. He always ran for them despite the fact I often sent them not down the path ahead but all over the place. My less than straight aim sent them over fences and gates, into gardens and porches, once even through an open car window! I'll never make an England bowler, but Fido didn't mind. If I threw, he chased. He didn't always retrieve the stick I'd thrown but no matter what he brought back I rewarded him generously with pieces of cheese. That was his absolutely favourite snack. He liked boiled eggs, sausage and biscuits too, but cheese was the winner. Luckily I quite often came by some as a kind of bonus at work.

From time to time I tried him on a more interesting name. I felt he warranted it but presumably he was happy with Fido as he never came scampering back until I gave in and called him that. I can't tell you the places I've clambered over and into whispering, 'Rufus come back' or 'here Harold'. To my utter embarrassment on a couple of occasions the property owners heard and joined in my search! On those occasions I quickly reverted to my dog's original name and took him away, all the time muttering awkward thanks and apologies. Often though there was no one at home, or at least no one heard and I got away with it.

Are you thinking I was a rubbish dog trainer? Or perhaps that I was a bumbling fool in other areas too. Can't blame you if so, as that's the impression I'd worked hard to create.

The man who has to run after his dog as it makes a beeline for those who'll bend over to stroke him is the man who can very easily slip a wallet or phone from a back pocket. The man who can explain his presence almost anywhere anytime is never suspected of casing the joint, or even being half-way through a burglary. Best of all, the man who has a dog which will run after a stick right in front of cameras and lights has someone to test out alarms and other security devices, and an excuse for them being triggered. And when that dog returns not with a stick, but a watch or bunch of keys he has a truly valuable partner in crime.

The only trouble with Fido was that of course he wasn't really a criminal; just a clever and loyal dog doing as his master had taught him. He didn't know he was stealing, just that he enjoyed bringing things to me. He had no idea we weren't welcome in the homes we visited late at night. To him the people we met in the park weren't marks or victims. To Fido they were lovely chums who fussed over him and gave him titbits. So when he found an old dear in a heap on her bedroom floor his reaction wasn't to grab what he could and get out. Instead he fetched the man who'd rescued him, clearly expecting me to show the same compassion to one of my own kind.

I didn't have a choice. Before I could call him away, the stupid mutt licked her face and she opened her eyes. Couldn't just leave her then, could I? She might be able to describe me, perhaps would even think I'd knocked her down, though it seemed pretty clear she'd simply fallen.

"Should I call an ambulance?" I asked.

"No… please. Back to bed… not hurt."

I scooped her up, put her back in her bed and pulled the quilt over her. She weighed nothing.

"When did you last eat?" I asked.

She didn't seem to know. When I had a look in her kitchen, I saw why. There had been cash in her bag. Elsewhere in the house display cabinets were stacked with expensive nicknacks, even after I'd taken my pick, but the fridge and kitchen cupboards were empty. That hadn't been the case at my last port of call.

When I'd taken a nice chunk off the slab of extra mature cheddar for Fido I'd seriously doubted it would even be missed. He'd already eaten that, but it wouldn't take me long to grab something else for the old woman. I shouldn't have needed to go. Clearly she could afford food and her neighbours were obviously capable of obtaining it. Even in huge places like this, with high walls and plenty of trees they'd surely realise others in the road were frail and vulnerable and hadn't been seen out lately?

When I got back, my 'victim' seemed to be asleep. Waving a bowl of warm lobster bisque under her nose woke her up. I hauled her into a sitting position, shoved cushions behind her to keep her there and dumped the tray on her lap. By the time I was back with a glass of fresh orange juice and piece of fruit cake, the soup was all gone and she looked much stronger.

"How did you find me?" she asked.

"Fido here must have heard you calling for help and led me to your back door. You should be more careful about locking it, but perhaps this time it's a good thing you didn't."

She had, but when I'd gone out on my mission of mercy I'd seen the key in the lock and undone it. Weak as she was, she wouldn't be certain she'd turned it.

"It's lucky you were passing," she murmured.

"Fido needs a lot of exercise and I prefer being out and about when it's quiet."

"I see."

I had an awful feeling she did and replaced her cash and crystal on my way out, taking instead the soup carton and cake wrapper.

First thing the next day, which is just after noon if you work the hours I did, I took the results of my labours to my usual fence, then went back to take Fido for a quick walk. I always kept him away from the sales side of things. There's no honour amongst thieves if turning someone in will reduce your sentence, so the less people who knew I didn't work alone the better.

Obviously I wasn't thinking straight, because I found myself back outside the old lady's house, with Fido wanting to go in. Returning to the scene of a crime is a big mistake. As I'd not been paying attention I had no idea who might have seen me. I glanced around and caught a glimpse of what looked horribly like a police car on the driveway of the house which was now missing a carton of very classy soup and a fruit cake, amongst other more valuable things. There was nothing for it, but to brazen it out. I knocked on the old lady's door.

After quite a time she opened the door, keeping it on the chain. She recognised Fido straight away, but was slower about letting us both in.

"Thought I'd see how you were and if there was anything I could get you," I explained as I accepted the seat she offered.

She sat on the sofa and patted the space next to her. I didn't even see Fido move; he just appeared by her side.

"It would be a big help if you could do a little shopping for me. I can pay you," she said as she stroked my dog's head.

"OK, sure I can do that."

She told me what she needed and gave me her purse. "Take as much as you want. I'm Daisy by the way."

"Right, um that's Fido and I'm Steve." I took half the amount I'd extracted the night before; still plenty for the shopping and my time. "Come on, Fido."

"They won't allow him in the shop, perhaps he had better stay with me?"

I was quite pleased when I had to tell Fido to 'stay' very firmly before he got the message. Despite the fuss she was making of him and the classy cushion he sat on, Fido wanted to be with me.

As I walked down to the bus stop I couldn't help wondering what was going on in Daisy's mind. Had she believed my story? Was she just being practical, or wanting the company when she suggested Fido stay, or was she holding him hostage against my return?

I got her food and worked myself up into a state. If I returned to find the police waiting for me, what would happen to Fido? There must be procedures; the police wouldn't just leave him to run wild. The rescue place would take him back I supposed, or maybe Daisy would take him in.

Fido wouldn't starve, but I flattered myself he'd miss his master and I knew I'd miss him. And there was a trust thing. He thought I'd rescued him and if I went off with the police he'd feel I'd abandoned him.

Thoughts of alternative ways to make a living crossed my mind. What though? My c.v. would read like a signed confession and can you imagine the references? 'Nice clean theft, no fingerprints left' or 'Very tidy job, didn't know he'd done it until I opened my wallet'.

There were no police with Daisy when I returned.

"Your dog is a marvel," she said. "I dropped the TV remote. It was the shock of the news about the burglary next door, I think. Dear Fido picked it up for me so I could switch it off. I don't want to hear about that kind of thing."

"He's very clever," I admitted. I also wondered if he was the only one.

"As you've brought the milk, how about we have a cup of tea and something to eat?"

"I'll see to it."

She must have been terribly hungry. Her previous night's weakness was presumably brought on by being half starved and she'd not have eaten again since the meal which revived her almost twelve hours earlier. I brought in a tray of sandwiches, pot of tea and selection of cakes.

"Tell me about yourself, Steve," Daisy invited.

"Not much to tell," I tried, but she was better at getting me to talk than any detective sergeant I've ever met. Sharp or not she can't have helped but notice a lot of gaps, especially when it came to work.

"If you're currently between jobs, perhaps you'd consider working for me?" she suggested.

"Doing what?" I asked.

"Shopping, some cleaning and house maintenance, work in the garden. General handyman I suppose. I can pay a reasonable amount and I'd be delighted to have Fido's company as you work."

I didn't know what to say, so ate another jam tart.

"There are quite a few things which need attention here and once this place is straight and I don't need you full time, I'll be in a position to recommend you to other people. I have several friends, all elderly and in need of some help like myself."

I looked over at Fido, with his head on her lap and tail wagging furiously. What choice did I have?

"All right then, yes. We could give that a try. Where would you like me to start?"

"I think by trimming those huge bushes which shield the house from the road. Do you know, I have this horrible fear that a burglar could lurk there unseen and we wouldn't want that, would we?"

I finished my tea and set to work.

"Oi! What are you doing?" a very pompous sounding voice demanded through the bushes.

For just a moment I froze in fear and dropped the shears I was holding. Fido retrieved them for me. That reminded me that things were very different from how they'd been just a few months earlier. It was three in the afternoon, not at night. I wasn't hiding from either the owner or passers-by.

"I asked you a question," Mr Pompous snarled. At the same time he moved to where he could see the partially trimmed shrub, the pile of clippings at my feet and shears in my hand.

I explained my current occupation, slowly and patiently, which seemed to do little to win him round.

Fido's yap alerted me to the presence of my new employer.

"That's looking better already, Steve," Daisy told me.

"I hope you got references for him?" Mr Pompous demanded.

"I tend to judge people by their actions and the company they keep," Daisy said. She stooped to fondle Fido's ears.

"You need to do better than that! You could be burgled like we were! They took all my cash, even raided the fridge…"

"And you came to warn me? How thoughtful," Daisy interrupted.

"Er, yes well I thought the police would…"

"So there's a burglar in the area," Daisy said. "We must be very careful." She looked me straight in the eye. "Isn't that right, Steve?"

I nodded my head and got back to clipping the shrub. She was right; I'm going to have to plan my jobs very carefully from now on. Well, if you have a four legged accomplice and two legged alibi, you'd be a fool not to make the most of them, wouldn't you?

18. Message From God

She knelt down to pick up the envelope which had just dropped onto the doormat and, with trembling hands, ripped it open and unfolded the sheet of paper.

She was pleased her hands trembled. Delighted her reaction combined anticipation with apprehension. Laughed aloud experiencing the powerful effect of a package of paper.

Naturally she knew no fear of poison pen letters!

The unmarried mother opposite had received one, the sinful life that girl led. Shocking! Reportedly upset when confronted with the truth, claimed widowhood, her husband killed in a car crash, that the visiting youths were her brothers. Oh the wicked lies people tell.

Mr and Mrs Somaranda were said to be good Christian souls. Do they believe occasional church visits disguise black magic and Voodoo rituals? The colour of their skin, and their letter, clearly proclaimed the truth.

Crippled Jennie Morrison, her deformity obviously a justified punishment from The Lord, had cried when she read hers. Good.

The boys next door denied allegations of benefit scrounging, cheating honest taxpayers. She understands aggressively bleached hair tattoos and body piercing, if they were working then it was by marketing drugs another letter accused.

No one knows who sends them, but they have unpleasant words to say about that person. Spiteful things. Phrases she'd shudder to hear in the same sentence as her name.

She continues. Sending the letters is her moral duty. Let he who is without sin cast the first stone! Never has she experienced the pleasures of the flesh. English born and bred, she attends Mass each Sunday.

That's why she is so shocked to look down and see, written in neatly printed red capitals, "STOP IT".

19. Pennies In Fountains

James made two mugs of tea and took them into the lounge.

Mum, who'd not long got in from work, looked up and smiled. "Oh, thank you, love" she said with as much appreciation as if he'd poured her a glass of champagne, or ordered a cream tea somewhere fancy. He wished he could do those things. She deserved them.

Mum returned her attention to the television. Usually she didn't watch much, but that had changed recently. The local news showed yet more footage about the dilapidated fountain in the square, which millionaire Lionel Baldwin was paying to have restored.

"It's nice to have some nice news," Mum said.

James agreed. Although he thought the money could have been put to better use, it would be good to see the central marble statue of three laughing children cleaned up, and water once again cascading over the repaired umbrellas. In the right light it would look magnificent, and he'd love the challenge of catching that movement and sparkle in a photograph.

After a bit about the fountain's history, the coverage switched to 'the great man himself' giving his motivational speech, all about starting small, forgetting your pride, working hard and getting results, just as he had with the market stall which became a chain of fashion stores. James, who'd heard it before, picked up his phone and scrolled through.

He found a couple of daft jokes which he told his mum, making her giggle. Not long afterwards he chucked his phone onto the coffee table.

"Careful," his mum said. "You'll damage it and I… they're not cheap."

Had she been going to say she couldn't afford another? Quite possibly, but she'd changed her mind. That was good of her, not to remind him that although he was twenty-one and theoretically able to fend for himself, she'd helped pay for the phone and provided the roof over his head.

"Sorry, I was just annoyed. My fault for looking at social media to start with," James said.

"There's nothing wrong with looking, love, but remember it doesn't show the whole story. People post holiday photos, special meals out, and new hair cuts. They brag about successes and sometimes share tragedies, but you don't see anything of their ordinary lives. The boring bits, the hard work which makes the glitter you see on the surface possible."

"Yeah, you're right. It wasn't that. I keep seeing quotes and things saying that if you want something hard enough you'll get it. That's rubbish, isn't it?"

Mum considered for a moment. "I suppose it's true in that we need to know what we want so we know where to focus our efforts. But no, just hoping for the best isn't enough. We have to work for what we want. And you do, I know you do."

"It's not enough though, is it?"

He'd worked hard at college, learning about photography. Mum had worked harder still, bringing him up on her own. When he got his qualification, she'd said it was worth it, that she was so very proud of him. He'd been looking forward to paying her back. She wasn't still paying for everything, but what he earned only just covered his share of the rent and household bills.

James had taken his portfolio to several photography companies and the local paper. They all said different versions of much the same thing – that he had talent and they'd like to employ him, but were sorry they simply couldn't afford another salary. He was offered work as a freelancer with several of them, but would need to supply all his own equipment, plus get himself to the locations. James did try, using what he already had. He got some great action shots during sports day at his old school, and was praised for the promotional pictures in the Indian restaurant, but most jobs weren't on bus routes and were further away than he could walk. The camera Mum had taken out a loan for, when he started college, was already out of date and the one lens didn't cover the range required for many of the assignments he'd otherwise have accepted. He sometimes had to make three attempts to restart his old laptop each time it crashed, making editing and submitting his digital photos stressful.

Thankfully he'd never been late turning in work, or lost important images, but he couldn't blame anyone when the small trickle of photography jobs he was offered dried up. James looked for alternative employment. Part-time work in a supermarket was all he could get, so that's what he took.

"At least I'll get staff discount on all your tea," he'd joked. It was 5% now and would rise when he'd been employed there for at least six months. James supposed he'd get to that point, but it wasn't much of an ambition. Not like the one, to become a professional photographer, it seemed he must give up on.

"Part-time is good. It will give you time to take photos and apply for something else," Mum had said.

Bless her, no matter what setbacks she suffered, she still had hope. James had tried to be the same. With Mum's help he'd bought the phone and used it to submit pictures to anywhere which might buy them. He'd sold a handful, but not enough to pay for a newer camera, or better lens. James, just as Lionel Baldwin advised, started small and worked hard. It wasn't enough – he wasn't getting results.

Others James had studied with had families rich enough to buy them cameras. One had a relative in the business who'd offered him a job. Then there was the girl who'd been at the right place at the right time to help a celebrity in distress and been rewarded with the commission to take his wedding photos, which had launched her career. They'd all worked, James couldn't say they hadn't, but they'd been lucky too. And that Lionel Baldwin, he'd been lucky, although he kept quiet about that!

Once James had seen how interested his mum was in the man, he'd looked him up, wondering if he could find a connection between them. He and Mum were similar in age, and the fact he was restoring the fountain in this particular town suggested that, like Mum, he'd begun life in the area. James had hoped they might have been schoolfriends, or even childhood sweethearts. Something which would persuade him to invest in the career of her son. James doubted it, as surely she'd have said so, but he'd hoped for that kind of luck. Maybe she'd kept quiet as she didn't realise it was the same person, or the story was embarrassing. For a short time he'd even fantasised that Lionel Baldwin was the father he'd never met.

What James had found, other than more detail about the same things the local paper and TV channel kept rehashing, was a short clip of Lionel, just after he made his fortune and came to public attention. When asked the secret of his success he'd laughed and said, "Pennies in fountains."

"You've been lucky, is that what you mean?" the reporter had asked.

Lionel had said, "We make our own luck, don't we?"

Since then he'd only ever talked about starting at the bottom, swallowing your pride, and working hard – but James knew different. Somewhere along the line, Lionel Baldwin had got lucky.

"You're looking thoughtful, love," Mum said.

"I was just thinking about that fountain." And wondering why Mum was quite so interested in it. "Did you ever meet him – Lionel Baldwin?"

"Not meet exactly, but I think I saw him a few times."

"Go on."

"It was in the library. I used to go in to read the fashion and beauty magazines. He always looked like he was studying. I thought he was daft using his weekends for schoolwork, but later I wished I'd worked harder."

"And that's why you always encouraged me to study. Thanks for doing that. I've got my qualification, and I'll find a way to use it, you see." He hugged her, then returned to his phone – not to scroll through social media this time. Both Mum and Lionel had said he should work hard. Lionel also said people made their own luck. That's what James was going to do – he'd work hard at getting lucky.

James was careful to stay within the law, and do nothing to arouse fear or cause annoyance, but he went everywhere

Lionel Baldwin made public appearances. Or at least all those which occurred when James wasn't working his shift in the supermarket. It took a lot of persistence, but eventually James got noticed. Lionel Baldwin sent his glamorous looking assistant to ask who James was working for and what it was they wanted.

"I'm working for myself, trying to make my own luck. I'll be happy to explain it all to Mr Baldwin if he's interested."

The assistant, looking unimpressed, turned and walked away.

"I'm starting with pennies in fountains," he called to the woman's back. He didn't know why, other than those words had caught his attention when he heard Lionel Baldwin say them.

After less than a minute's conversation with her boss, the assistant returned. "You may explain yourself to Mr Baldwin if you wish, but please keep it concise. He's on his way to an important meeting."

"Thank you. I will…" She was again walking away, so James rushed after her.

James was shown into the back of a large and very comfortable car, then left alone. Just as he was thinking he was wasting his time, the assistant, Lionel Baldwin, and a chauffeur, all got in with James.

"Tell me your story, young man," Lionel invited.

James told him almost everything. Although, as he'd agreed, he used as few words as possible, he hadn't quite finished when the car stopped and the chauffeur held open the door for Lionel.

"We're here, sir," Lionel's assistant prompted. 'Here' being another town, over ten miles away.

"What is it you want from me?" Lionel asked James.

"A little luck. A start like you had." Then realising he was out of time so needed to be direct, said, "A loan of a thousand pounds. It's nothing to you, work on that fountain is costing many times as much, but it would mean everything to me."

"Sir, we really must go."

"Take him wherever he needs to be," Lionel directed the chauffeur. He and his assistant left.

"Home please." As James gave his address he was grateful that at least he wouldn't either have to pay bus fare or walk for hours.

As the chauffeur drove James home, he asked if a thousand pounds really would make that much difference.

"Yes. I asked the companies who offered me the job, and one will still take me on as a freelancer if I can get where they send me, and take a camera with me. The thousand pounds would get me second-hand kit and a pushbike. Nothing fancy, but enough to do the job. I'm good, and I work hard. With a small start like that, I'll make it." All he wanted was a tiny bit of luck, so he could follow the advice Lionel Baldwin gave in all his TV interviews.

"Good luck, lad," the chauffeur said outside the flats where James lived with his mum.

"Thanks." Although his situation hadn't changed, that luck seemed further away than ever. Unless the chauffeur was as sympathetic as he seemed, and put in a good word for him with Mr Baldwin.

Two days later a courier delivered an envelope, containing a thousand pounds in cash. And a month after that, James was sent to photograph the unveiling of the newly restored fountain. Lionel Baldwin was, of course, there to make a speech. The assistant he'd previously met beckoned him forward. At first James thought that was so he could get better shots, but after he'd taken a few, she asked James to join her and her boss.

Lionel gestured towards James. "This young man came to see me recently. He reminded me of myself, a good few years ago. I started, as I've said before, with very few advantages in life. I worked hard and became a success. For some, hard work is enough. My assistant here started as the office junior, now she runs my schedule and one day I'll have to manage without her because she'll be snapped up by a huge corporation to keep them running smoothly. But for others, hard work alone isn't enough. They need something more." He looked toward James.

"Luck?"

"Indeed some are lucky and get given what they need, or are able to earn or make it, but that's not always the case. As is well documented, I started with a market stall. A humble beginning but even when your stall isn't official so there's no rent to pay, and you borrow your mum's kitchen table to set it up, you need something to sell. I didn't have anything, and no money to buy it. All I had was a penny." He held one up.

"I was going to throw it in the fountain, and wish for the luck some of us need. I saw all the other pennies in there — and more valuable coins too. I wondered about all the good luck asked for, the wishes made and if any had come true. Then I swallowed my pride, jumped in and scooped up all that cash."

There were gasps from the audience.

"By restoring the fountain now, I hope you'll agree I'm repaying the unofficial loan."

There were nods at that, and James wondered what would have happened to the money if Lionel hadn't taken it, and what would happen to the coins which would inevitably end up in the new one.

"We'll skip through my rise to fame and fortune, to when I met James. He explained how, just like me back in the day, he needed a relatively small sum of money to get started but, again like me, it was money he just didn't have. He also pointed out that it was a very small percentage of the cost of restoring this beautiful fountain. That got me thinking." Lionel nodded to his assistant.

She held up what looked like a charity collection box. On the front were the words 'Pennies In Fountains'.

"I'm setting up a charity," Lionel continued. "And have donated a sum of money to help those who, like I did, and like James did, need a start in life. Any local young person my apply for a grant to buy equipment, or pay for training, or anything else which will allow them to work hard and make their own luck. I urge you to throw any spare change you have, not into this fountain, but in here."

The assistant began moving through the crowd, who dropped coins and a few notes into the collection box.

That was a year ago. James has been hired to photograph an event celebrating the hundredth grant made by the Pennies In Fountains charity. He isn't yet rich or famous, but has impressed his employers enough that they've offered him a salaried position, and supplied him with a long range lens.

He's taken his mum out to dinner and ordered her a glass of champagne. It's a small step towards repaying his massive debt to her, and he'll continue his efforts to do that for the rest of his life. There's another debt which he can't pay immediately, but on which he can make a start. When the assistant walks round with the collection box, James slips in one hundred pounds, and silently promises he'll do the same nine more times. There are plenty of things he'd like to buy with the thousand pounds he originally received from Lionel Baldwin, but he doesn't absolutely need it now. He wants it to go to someone who does. Someone who needs the luck he's had.

20. Sleeping Witness

Rachel was choking. Before her panic woke Tim she realised it was a nightmare. She calmed her breathing and tried to get back to sleep.

A week later she had another nightmare. Like the first, but more vivid. She felt as though someone was forcing tablets and water into her mouth and she was trying not to swallow them.

"You OK?" Tim asked drowsily.

"Just a dream."

The dream stayed with her. She stopped taking her multivitamin, sipped her drinks very slowly.

It happened again. She saw a man leaning over her. Felt his hand on her face, over her mouth. She knew he meant her harm.

"What's wrong?" Tim asked, stroking her cheek.

In terror she lashed out, then realised what she was doing. "I'm sorry. Living in a house where someone was killed is taking more getting used to than I thought."

"Another dream?"

She explained it. Then seeing his worried expression said, "We did the right thing buying the house. The dreams must be because I'm unsettled by the move. They'll stop soon."

The house had been cheap because of its history. It had been sold twice since the murder, but new owners never stayed long. Just enough time to start removing fixtures and fittings.

"Are you sure it doesn't bother you?" Tim asked before they made an offer.

"I can't say I like the idea, but it was years ago and the killer is in prison, isn't he?"

"He is," Tim had assured her.

"Then there's nothing to worry about. The only uncomfortable feeling I'm getting is of something unfinished. You can see why."

He'd nodded. "If we buy it, we'll practically be camping for a while."

"I don't mind that."

She hadn't, nor the hard work involved in making their new home a pleasant place to live. The nightmares were a different matter. They happened every night now and left her anxious all the time. No way would she be able to visit the dentist, or have a beautician touch her face. She couldn't even eat her favourite mints which looked like tablets. At work she'd had to swap desks away from the cooler as seeing anyone approach with a glass of water was terrifying.

"How did Mrs Jones die?" she asked Tim.

"You said you didn't want to know the details."

"Only because I thought my imagination might run away with me. It's doing that anyway."

"Actually I didn't ask, for the same reason, but I expect we can find out online."

A search brought up a great deal of information, and several photos.

"That's him, the man from my dream!"

"You must have seen it in the papers or something when it happened," Tim said. "Look, it says her doctor killed her with sleeping tablets."

They read an account of the case. A distant cousin, Jack Jones, had been staying with old Mrs Jones. He'd called Doctor Robinson out in the night, saying she was struggling to breathe. The doctor claimed there was nothing really wrong. "She's just very old. She could go at any time, and there's nothing to be done about it."

In the morning she was dead. As Doctor Robinson had been on call all night it was his colleague who was summoned. That doctor had attended Mrs Jones in the past and was perfectly willing to sign the death certificate until Jack said Doctor Robinson had given the deceased some medication. "He gave her a pill to help her sleep and asked me to fetch more water to help her swallow it."

In case that meant the lady might have had something other than old age wrong with her, Doctor Robinson was asked about this.

"He's mistaken. She hadn't been prescribed sleeping pills and naturally I don't carry them round with me. Besides, she was asleep the whole time I was there."

Doctor Robinson's colleague had no choice but to request an autopsy. This revealed Mrs Jones had swallowed a lot of sleeping tablets. The same type Doctor Robinson had prescribed for several of his patients, and which he himself sometimes used.

When it was discovered Mrs Jones had left everything to the doctor, he was accused, and then found guilty, of murder. Jack said he thought she'd left all her money to a charity, but her solicitor revealed she'd never done so and the previous will had named Jack. As he was her only relative, and being found guilty of her murder meant Doctor Robinson couldn't inherit, everything went to Jack.

"I really have been dreaming of her murder," Rachel said when she and Tim finished reading.

"Like I said, you must have read about it."

"Look at the date it happened."

"Where does it say… Oh, your birthday!"

"Do you think I'd forget that, if I'd heard about it before?"

"It seems unlikely… But why would Mrs Jones haunt you and not the doctor?"

"Because it isn't him I see in my dreams, it's her cousin Jack. That feeling I've had, of something not finished? She wants me to reveal the truth."

"I don't know about that, but I see the nightmares will continue until you're sure the right man is behind bars."

They did more than continue, they increased. Rachel was certain the old lady was doing her best to communicate.

Rachel contacted the detective who'd investigated the case, explaining she was having nightmares. "Why were you so sure the doctor killed her?" she asked.

"To tell the truth I wasn't, but someone did. There was no packaging for those pills anywhere in the house, and no innocent explanation for anyone giving her them and hiding the evidence. The doctor had a very strong motive, and there was Jack's statement against him."

"Sleeping pills can't be that hard to get hold of, and it was actually Jack who gained by her death."

"I know, and that came up at the trial. The prosecution said that as Jack thought the money would go to charity he didn't have a motive. He could have been lying, but the jury believed him."

"I know it was Jack. How do I persuade you to reopen the case?"

"I'm already halfway to believing you, but we need evidence."

A few days later, as Rachel was replacing the curtain tracking in their bedroom, she dropped a screw. It fell between the floorboards.

"We're going to have to take one up."

"It's not worth it. They'll be almost impossible to shift and there are plenty more screws," Tim said.

"That's what Jack would have thought if he'd dropped a pill."

They eventually raised a floorboard, discovering dust, the screw, an old coin, two yellowing playing cards and an empty medicine blister pack.

Rachel rang the detective. "I've found your evidence. You'll have to test it of course, but I know it once held sleeping tablets, and has Jack's fingerprints on it."

That night, Rachel dreamed again. She was free at last, with nothing left unfinished. She floated gently upwards, towards a bright, beautiful light. She woke for a moment, whispered, "Goodbye, Mrs Jones," then went back to sleep.

21. A Nice Little Hobby

I've always needed to be active. Stimulated. It's not good for me to get restless or lonely. Walking in nature helps I've discovered, since starting my new hobby.

It's soothing to stretch my legs, breathe fresh air and feel part of something. An aimless walk on my own isn't the same. It's much better with company and a reason to be there. Any walk builds an appetite of course, but my new interest also helps satisfy my hunger.

Recently I've been volunteering for manhunts.

I don't mean as a vigilante hunting down desperate criminals, but helping out when a person goes missing. When people come together to search for sweet little Jenny, tearaway Tim, or senile old Uncle Derek, I'm part of it. Their emotions almost become mine. Hope of course, and fear. Most people are there because of a mix of the two. There's worry over what will be missed and what might be found. Even joy sometimes, if there's a clue. It's hard to describe – exhilarating and exhausting and unforgettable.

It does me so much good to see that people care. Not just the family, but the shop owner who sold Jenny the sweets which mean that even if she's not found for years, dental records will identify her. Or those who jumped out the way of Tim and his scooter, or drank with Derek when he could still remember what his usual actually was.

The first time I got involved was almost accidental. I was driving along a quiet road, part way through what had previously been my only little hobby, when I noticed a dozen or so cars parked on the verge and scores of people huddled together, listening to a police officer. One of his colleagues waved me down and produced a photo.

"Have you seen this boy?"

"Poor kid's missing? Can I help?"

Human searchers, and trained dogs, were spread thinly over rugged and beautiful moorland.

Of course we didn't find him.

The mother hugged me when I expressed genuine certainty her son was close by. She was so grateful for my help and words of comfort I was rather sorry I had to drive away with the kid in the boot and dump him elsewhere.

Now I make sure those I take never see my face. Hunting is much more fun when even I don't know if they'll be found dead or alive.

22. Make Or Break

Richard had guessed the woman he was about to interview as senior waitress was the same Fran Adams he'd dated as a teenager. The moment he saw her, he had no doubts. Twenty years on those bright blue eyes, beguiling smile and silky raven hair were just the same.

"Please take a seat," he invited.

Richard studied Fran's application form. It was impressive – she'd trained in first aid, food hygiene, and marketing, all skills which would be useful to him. The glowing references proved her to be likeable and reliable.

He couldn't ignore the fact she was an attractive woman, nor dismiss the memory of kissing that smiling mouth. Why the heck had he dumped her? Oh yes, because his family owned this restaurant which was doing well back then and she just had her mum who cleaned toilets in the shopping centre. Pure snobbery that was and not even his own. Richard's friends made sarky comments and he'd cared so much about their opinion he'd heartlessly and very publicly dumped a lovely girl who'd done nothing wrong.

He couldn't believe Fran hadn't recognised him, but she'd not given any sign. He hoped she was being tactful, and not still so upset she didn't want to recall the past.

Richard ran through the formalities then said, "Please tell me why you think you'd be suitable for this job."

"I've worked in lots of restaurants, great ones and not so great. I've seen what makes them succeed or fail, and know what will make or break this one."

As Fran continued it became clear she'd be perfect for the job. Richard needed someone perfect. He'd sunk all his money into reviving the family business. He had to make it work as he'd lose everything and greatly disappoint his beloved grandparents if it failed.

They'd created a reputation for exceptional food and service. His father didn't have their passion, so quality and profits both slumped, until Grandad had said, "Do it right or don't do it at all."

Now it was down to Richard to get it right, or admit he couldn't and that the place must close. His grandparents were helping all they could, mainly with advice.

"Get good staff, that's they key," Grandad said.

"There's nothing wrong with pretty waitresses," Nanna added, "but you need someone well trained and experienced to take charge and keep everything running properly."

Fran fitted the bill perfectly. Richard wanted to offer her the job, but there was something he had to clear up first. "Don't you recognise me?" he asked.

"Of course I do. Part of being a good waitress is remembering people."

"Things didn't end well between us. Will that be a problem if you work for me?"

"Of course not," Fran said. "Another part of being a good waitress is being pleasant and doing my best for people, even those I may not like, or who don't deserve it," Fran said.

"Right. I see."

Fran laughed. "Don't look so worried, Richard. I'm not holding a grudge. Our short romance was a long time ago and we were kids. I've long since moved on. It's not like you were the love of my life and left me emotionally scarred."

Well, that put a dent in his ego! Still, he was glad he'd not seriously hurt her.

"Treat me fairly and pay me well, and there won't be a problem," Fran said.

"Deal!"

Fran worked hard training new waitresses and keeping things running smoothly as they prepared for the formal, grand reopening. She had excellent ideas. It was her suggestion they 're-opened' despite never having completely closed.

"You want to make it clear that things have moved on from the way they were the last few years and you've gone back to how it was in the glory days."

Richard saw the sense of that, plus the benefits of the publicity which a big event, with specially invited guests, could bring. He listened to her advice about where to position tables, lighting and table decorations to make things easier for staff and more comfortable for customers.

The re-opening event was going perfectly. Every one of the influential people on the guest list he and Fran had drawn up were there, including two quite well known sports personalities and a minor TV star. There had been a short, and entertaining, speech by a popular local comedian, followed by live music and complimentary wine and canapés for as many people as they could squeeze in. That had been expensive, but many of those who attended that part of the evening made bookings before they left.

Now it was just the diners left. They included the VIP guests, but also plenty of ordinary paying customers, who'd hopefully tell everyone they knew about the experience. One couple in particular had spent a lot of money. They'd ordered all the most expensive dishes and the priciest champagne. Richard didn't recognise them, but saw Fran keeping a careful eye and personally checking what was brought to them before it reached the table, so guessed they were important.

"You've done wonderfully," Nanna told Richard, as his grandparents prepared to leave. "We couldn't have done better ourselves."

"We're very proud of you," Grandad said. "You've made the restaurant great again." They slipped away, but most people were finishing their dessert and ordering coffee and liqueurs.

Fran was still being brilliant, charming customers, soothing staff, even popping out to check on the parking situation. Richard had been so busy with his own charm offensive he'd hardly had time to speak to her. That wasn't right. He should let her know how much he appreciated all she'd done to make the evening such a wonderful success. How much he appreciated her full stop.

As he headed in her direction, Richard saw that the female half of the big spending couple had left the table, presumably to visit the ladies. The man ordered brandy – the kind which cost more than a whole bottle of champagne for a single measure and he asked for a double!

Richard didn't think things could be going any better. Everyone seemed happy and relaxed. He'd received lots of compliments about the food, atmosphere and attention to detail. Richard was sure numerous good reports of the restaurant would be made, and that bookings would soon flood in.

His thoughts were interrupted by an awful sound – something halfway between a loudly gurgling drain and a scream. The door to the bathroom area flew open with a crash and a woman staggered through. Richard could only tell from her dress that she was the woman who'd ordered the best of everything. Her face was vivid red and swollen, her eyes bulged. She clutched at her throat, gasping for breath and continuing to make that awful high-pitched gurgling.

"Let me through! My wife is suffering anaphylactic shock," her husband yelled as he rushed to her side. People cried out and knocked things over as they either tried to get out the way, or get a better look.

"There must have been nuts in her food, even though we said she's allergic. Make way, I must get her to hospital before it's too late!" Supporting, almost carrying, his wife he went out, shouting orders to let the hospital know they were on the way.

Richard was sickened by those taking photos on their phones and shocked by what was happening. He must have misheard Fran, but as she raced out after the couple it sounded as though she instructed a waitress to make up their bill and bring it out.

Quite a crowd had gathered and there was uproar when it was discovered the couple's car was blocked in. Richard saw with horror that the car stopping them leave was Fran's own vehicle. Surely she didn't plan to delay the emergency dash to hospital by presenting their bill? That would be heartless…

Richard felt cold and a little dizzy as he realised what was happening. Fran had lied about not holding a grudge over the way he'd dumped her and was getting her revenge. He wasn't sure if she'd deliberately invited someone with a nut allergy, or if she'd only got the idea when the woman mentioned it, but obviously Fran had used that fact to her advantage. That's why she'd paid so much attention to what they were given – she'd needed an opportunity to add something to the woman's dessert which would trigger this awful reaction.

"I know what will make or break this restaurant," she'd said – and she'd decided to break him!

Richard tried to see through the crowd, some of whom were filming the action on their phones. The poisoned woman had collapsed and was no longer gasping for breath. Did that mean she was dead already? He could see the headlines now. He'd be ruined.

"Nobody panic," Fran said. "I'm a qualified first aider." She knelt by the stricken woman, then held up a napkin smeared with red. "It's make-up and her cheeks are stuffed with cotton wool."

The woman scrambled to her feet and tried to run, but the crowd of onlookers made that impossible.

"As you can see she's fine," Fran continued. "Although that might change when the police arrest the pair of them for attempting to obtain a free meal by deception, stealing the salt and pepper pots, public disorder, assault and probably lots more."

By then the police had arrived. They acted quickly, to cheers from the crowd who'd greatly enjoyed the drama once they realised an innocent person wasn't about to die.

All the action was caught on film – this was going to be great publicity!

It was another hour before the remaining customers and guests finished their meals, paid their bills where appropriate, and the restaurant could close for the night.

"Fran, I must apologise. I doubted you," Richard said. "But how did you know?"

"I'd seen this couple in action once before. They got away with it then, but when I asked after her at the hospital I discovered she'd never been admitted and realised it was a scam. I couldn't let them get away with it here – your business would have been ruined if people thought a customer was almost killed by your food. I made sure the waitress asked if they had special dietary requirements. The couple denied it, but I still double-checked their food didn't contain nuts, so I'd know for sure any reaction wasn't a genuine one."

"I don't know what to say. Thank you doesn't seem enough. Perhaps a pay rise?"

Fran shook her head. "I said that if you treated me fairly and paid me well, we wouldn't have a problem, and you already pay me a good wage."

"I didn't treat you fairly by not trusting you."

"I don't blame you for falling for that couple's antics. They acted it out well. I bet they've done something similar lots of times, probably getting away with more than dinner on occasions."

Richard thought she was probably right, but that wasn't the main thing on his mind. "The way I treated you in the past…"

"Was a long time ago and like I said, I moved on. Tonight though… I've been on my feet for hours – even longer than we expected, and hardly had a chance to eat. What I think would be fair is for you to say I can have tomorrow night off and you'll take me, out and someone else can bring me my food and pour my wine."

Richard, as he was learning to do whenever Fran had a good idea, did exactly as she'd suggested.

23. A Fresh Page

Melanie, would-be journalist at The Daily Update, slumped in her chair feeling defeated. She was furious with Gilbert, or sir, as he liked her to call him. He was the features editor responsible for politics, entertainment and celebrity gossip and her immediate boss, so she did her best to keep him sweet – within reason.

Every day he picked more and more faults. "Too wishy-washy," he'd say, or "Too opinionated." If he found so much as a misplaced comma he'd declare the entire piece unreadable. Occasionally, in trying to put right her alleged mistakes he'd 'accidentally' delete the entire piece and expect Melanie to start again. "And quickly! We can't publish a blank page, can we?"

Of course she kept back ups. She wasn't as stupid as he thought, but his claim she was devious wasn't unfounded. He'd banned her from keeping copies of the articles she wrote for him on her work computer, but she got around that by emailing them to her machine at home. As Gilbert was quite capable of searching her sent messages she took care to only do this in her lunch break and to label the documents as though they were something personal. He wouldn't be worried about breaching her confidentiality, but she doubted he'd open a document which seemed to be a record of her monthly cycle.

Every day he gave her more work.

"You are my assistant, aren't you?" he'd bark if she even thought of querying the workload, or the fact he was taking another afternoon off to play golf.

"Your research assistant," she'd remind him when she felt brave enough.

It didn't do any good. "Act like it," he'd snap. "Get that written up before you leave tonight. I'll read it through in the morning and I don't want to see any more of your stupid mistakes."

She'd stay late most nights. She had to in order to do both her own job and Gilbert's. He'd turn up mid-morning, somehow having enough time to read her work and find a fault to point out just as the main editor popped in to check all was well.

The editor would pat her hand. "Don't you worry, Flower. With Gilbert showing you how things are done, you'll soon master grammar and develop your vocabulary."

Melanie was often tempted to vent her feelings with a few choice words from her already extensive vocabulary. But the editor had a very high opinion of Gilbert and very old-fashioned views of women in the workplace. Swearing, ranting, or even polite complaints wouldn't do her any favours.

Sometimes Gilbert smiled fondly and uttered a few words of meagre praise in front of the editor. The only times he ever did. "She's quite good at using the internet now," he'd say. Or, "Melanie managed to charm an interesting quote from the Mayor of London yesterday." Such remarks were designed to show she still had a long way to go, and her main skill was flirting with sources.

The plan, when she'd accepted the job, was that Melanie would gather background information for his pieces.

Gilbert was supposed to write the articles, and show her how it was done. At first that's what happened. Then he'd given Melanie a little more responsibility. She was to phone experts, witnesses and interested parties to obtain the quotes he needed. Melanie agreed as it allowed her to build a network of contacts.

Before long, Melanie was told to write notes for Gilbert's articles. Again she'd not minded as it was great practice and it gave her a thrill to see some of her sentences in finished pieces. Gradually Gilbert had sloped more and more of his work onto Melanie, until she was doing almost everything. All Gilbert did was take the praise and pay, and pass any blame for inaccuracies onto her.

Time and again she attempted to get recognition for her work, but was always fobbed off.

That's why, when Gilbert got a pay rise as a reward for the improvement in the quality of his pieces, Melanie was livid and found the courage to assert herself. "If I'm to write all these articles, my name should appear alongside yours," she'd insisted.

Gilbert had looked shocked and then thoughtful. "Yes, you're right – you really do deserve some credit. Both our names together might confuse readers though. What we'll do is to put just your name on a few pieces. How's that?"

"Thank you, sir," she said, smiling very sweetly to hide her suspicion it was some kind of trick.

She was right not to trust him, but not in the way she'd expected. Having long ago guessed his password of Gilbert15Greight she checked his sent messages. To her surprise several short articles really did carry her byline. Had she misjudged him?

A quick read through showed she hadn't. The few pieces with her name on had a huge number of errors, both in the content and way it was presented. Errors which she knew weren't present in the versions she'd sent him. There wasn't time for her to correct them. Well, there was, but not time to do that and write up Gilbert's big piece which she'd been researching for weeks.

Gilbert wasn't there when Melanie arrived the next day. That wasn't unusual. When the editor arrived Gilbert still hadn't turned up, which was.

"I need his article now," the editor said. "I hope it's ready?"

"Oh, I'm sure it is. Gilbert would be here working on it otherwise."

"You're right of course. Be a dear and bring it up on his computer, that's if you can?"

"I can try."

She was just about to type in Gilbert's password when he arrived. "What's going on?" he demanded.

"The girl was just telling me your big piece is ready and was about to find it for me."

"Leave that will you, Melanie?"

"If you're sure, sir?"

"It's such an important piece I want to just run my eye over it one final time before I release it."

"Hear that, Flower? Those are the words of a conscientious journalist."

Melanie returned to her own desk and waited. The editor left and Gilbert opened up the document. "There'd better not be any mistakes in this."

"There aren't, I promise you." How could there be when it was a blank page?

"What the hell is this?" Gilbert demanded.

"Every word you've written on the subject."

"It's blank!" he yelled.

"Exactly."

"You've not done your job!"

"Yes, Gilbert, I have. I've done all the necessary research, which is what I'm paid to do. I even obtained useful quotes despite that not technically being my job. It's all there in your in tray."

"But you've not written the article!"

"As I said, that's not my job." She let him sweat for a moment. "Don't worry I have written it."

"Then send it to me now!"

"I don't think so, Gilbert. Either you send in the empty page with your name on it, or I send in MY article with MY name on it."

He was defeated and he knew it. "Go on then."

First she rang the editor. "I'm sorry to say I was mistaken and Gilbert has not written his article."

"What are you talking about, girl?"

"I have a name and you will agree to use it on the article, or you'll have not one but three empty pages."

"Well, I…"

"What's more, after you've read it, you'll reconsider whether it's Gilbert or myself who deserves that pay rise."

"It seems I have no choice but to agree… Melanie. But I will not be swayed by one piece. I shall compare it with Gilbert's articles in the same issue."

"Excellent idea. I'm sending you the article now."

Once she'd done so she turned to Gilbert, who was looking quite smug. "I noticed you'd done a little work on the articles which you'd agreed could carry my byline."

"Just trying to help."

"That's sweet of you, but I couldn't possibly take the credit for your efforts, so I took my name off, put yours back on and re-sent them with apologies for your mistake."

"Did you change anything else?" He'd stopped looking smug and looked decidedly worried – as he should.

"No. Every error you introduced is still there for the boss, and everyone else, to read."

Gilbert slumped in his chair looking utterly defeated. She knew the feeling so well she almost felt sorry for him.

24. Death By Red Velvet

When the call came about a potential murder, during a Red Velvet baking contest, it sounded like a game.

"Mr Baker in the kitchen with the egg whisk?" Detective Patrick Ryan quipped.

"Hope the cakes weren't damaged. I'm planning on taking a huge slice as evidence!" his partner Wilma Sanchez replied.

"Don't spoil your appetite for tonight's barbecue. I can almost taste that smokey sauce the chief inspector uses…"

"Stop talking about it," Wilma instructed. "I can't interview suspects when I'm drooling!"

Hunger and humour deserted them on seeing the body of competition judge Cindi Longe, slumped over a desk, pen in hand. In front of her were four wonderful looking Red Velvet cakes, each with a small slice removed, and a glass of water.

"No sign of a struggle. Maybe it was a heart attack?" Patrick suggested.

Wilma would have loved him to be right, but knew he wasn't. "I don't think so. Her skin colour would be very different and I can't imagine she'd still be holding the pen as though she'd just fallen asleep. I suspect poisoning."

"Suicide?" Patrick suggested. "There's a sheet of paper under the body. If we're lucky it's a suicide note and we'll make it to the chief's barbecue on time and with this thing solved."

"That's no suicide note. It's the winner's certificate," said a voice from the doorway.

"And you are?" Patrick demanded.

"Lilian Marsh, judge's assistant. It was me who found her and called you."

"Can you talk us through what happened?" Wilma asked.

Lilian explained the process as the competitors baked and iced their cakes. The descriptions of chocolate, vanilla and the rich cream cheese topping made Wilma hungry again. She was tempted to tell Lilian to skip ahead, but needed to be sure there hadn't been an opportunity for tampering with the cakes. "Are the contestants watched the whole time?"

"Yes. Well…"

"Go on," Wilma urged.

"Cindi could only concentrate on one person at a time and the bakers themselves would be paying attention to what they were doing, not watching the others very closely."

They would if winning the competition was their reason to be there, Wilma thought, but not if they had murder in mind. "Was everyone of a similar standard?"

"Quite close. They all had to get through two rounds of heats."

It was still possible the murderer was one of the bakers, but if so the crime would have been planned well in advance. The quick solution Wilma and Patrick hoped for was seeming very unlikely.

"Could anyone have come in from outside?" Lilian asked.

"The door isn't locked, but I'm sure I would have noticed. Although I don't judge, I'm on hand in case Cindi wants me for anything."

"What about… um, comfort breaks?" Patrick asked.

"There's time for that when the cakes are cooked and cooling. Nobody left at any other time."

"And could anyone have accessed the cakes then?"

"Not without being seen. Most of the time bakers remained in the kitchen area preparing their toppings. Some did look at the other cakes then, but it's not the done thing to get too close so it would have been noticed."

"And you yourself stayed in the room?"

"I left once, but not at the same time as Cindi."

It didn't seem likely anyone could have poisoned a cake without someone seeing, not unless it was the one they'd baked.

"What happed after the icing was finished?" Lilian asked.

"The bakers left. I helped Cindi carry the cakes into her office for judging, then cleaned everything up. From your questions I guess you suspect there was something in one of the cakes which shouldn't have been there. I didn't notice anything unusual in the rubbish bins, but of course there were lots of containers which held different powders; flour, icing sugar, raising agent, and bottles of flavouring and things like that so I might not have noticed."

Wilma nodded, glad that it wouldn't be her job to go through the industrial sized rubbish bin she and Patrick had parked next to when they arrived. "When did you discover she was dead?"

"I brought her a fresh glass of water and…" Lilian shuddered.

"And nobody except you, the deceased, and the entrants were present at the venue, as far as you know?"

"Not once the competition started. Before that some friends and family helped carry in equipment and wished contestants well. This was the final, so the winner's announcement was supposed to be televised, but Cindi changed the date at the last minute so that fell through. It was just the four of them."

"You think a contestant killed Ms Longe?" Patrick asked.

"I'm afraid I do, yes. Not George Brown or Sandy Watkins. George has retired and had to be talked into entering at all."

"Cindi asked him especially?"

"I asked him. I knew the competition would be taken more seriously if it wasn't all women. Four men entered. Only George made it to the final, but he didn't put in a great deal of effort. You may have noticed one looks a little plainer than the others?"

Lilian and Patrick both nodded, although they'd all looked pretty fancy to Wilma.

"It would have done him no particular good to win and I don't think he wanted the publicity."

"Did Sandy Watkins want to win?" That name rang a bell somewhere in Wilma's memory.

"I'm sure she did, but only as a matter of pride really. She's standing as a candidate to be our local MP. Her ambitions aren't connected with baking. Winning might have given her good publicity, but…"

"Being connected with a murder wouldn't? I agree." Sandy couldn't be dismissed altogether, but seemed a very unlikely killer, especially as Wilma had now recalled that her campaign promises all involved things to make local people feel safer.

"What about the other two?" Patrick asked.

"I can't really believe either of them are killers, but they were counting on the TV publicity and were furious when they learned it wasn't happening. Laura-Beth has a new book out, a murder mystery set in a coffee shop. Maybelle owns a store selling cookery equipment."

Both sounded like strong motives, but would they have had time to act?

"When and why was the date changed?" Wilma asked.

"Two weeks ago. Since then both Maybelle and Laura-Beth have rung and emailed me complaining about it and asking me to use my influence to get Cindi to change it back. I don't have that kind of influence and wouldn't have used it if I had."

"And the reason?" Patrick prompted.

"Cindi didn't actually say, but I do know she'd arranged to go into the TV studio and talk through the results instead. I expect she'd have mentioned her cookery school too. It may have been to her advantage to have all the focus on her, but I can't see it would have made much difference."

"How about you? Would you have benefitted from the publicity?"

"Me on TV? I couldn't care less," Lilian said. "The date change worked in my favour as it happens. It's my birthday and both Maybelle and Sandy said I could keep their cakes as a birthday treat. Oh dear, I suppose they're evidence now?"

"I'm afraid so," Wilma said.

As a medical examiner attended the body, and the cakes and water glass were taken for analysis, Patrick and Wilma interviewed the contestants in turn.

They all denied tampering with their own or anyone else's cakes, and said they'd not gone into the judge's office at any time. They were all convincing.

George Brown had a slightly odd attitude to the murder. "It's not fair. I didn't want any publicity. Lilian promised it would be a low key affair, then that silly woman Cindi goes and gets herself killed!"

Although not sympathetic he was helpful, providing detailed recollections of the event and all that remained of the ingredients he'd used, including some cream cheese toping he'd saved to give his grandchildren.

Sandy Watkins was much more tactful, but it was still clear the murder was a disadvantage to her. She also seemed genuinely sorry the competition judge had died, and willing to help in any way.

Both the other suspects freely admitted to annoyance over the loss of TV coverage and that the murder could be a good thing for them.

"No doubt about it, my book sales will go up now I've been involved in a real murder," Laura-Beth said. "But although I plot murders I haven't committed one."

Maybelle too admitted the publicity might be good for business. "But that doesn't give me a motive. Unlike Laura-Beth's book, my store and Lilian's bakery would have been much better off with TV coverage that didn't involve murder. Poor Lilian, what a thing to happen on her birthday!"

A call came through to say preliminary results showed Ms Longe had indeed been poisoned, but there was no trace of the substance responsible in the water glass, the cakes, or any of the ingredients gathered from contestants.

Gloomily Patrick said, "I'd better call the chief and say we're not going to make the barbecue."

"Call him yes, but say we'll be there soon and with the case solved."

"You might have solved it, but you're going to have to explain it to me," Patrick said.

"Lilian Marsh was the killer."

"Why?"

"The publicity would have done her bakery as much good as it would have the others, but I'd guess the dismissive way Cindi treated her was what pushed her into it. If the contest had been televised she'd have been seen in action. I doubt she'd have got any mention had Cindi lived to go into the studio, but Lilian was the one who did all the work. It was her who persuaded people to enter and who they complained to about the date change. Three of the contestants knew it was her birthday, so it's hard to believe Cindi didn't, yet she still picked this as the day Lilian would do all the clearing up whilst she was the one to eat cakes."

"That gives her a motive, but how did she do it?"

"As the judge's assistant she'd known in advance that the event wasn't going to be televised, and had time to get the poison."

"So did everyone else."

"Yes, but little opportunity to add poison to anything Cindi would consume, and none to dispose of the evidence afterwards."

"I see what you mean. If it had been in the cakes or water glass, we'd have found traces. But then how…?"

"When Lilian helped carry the cakes into the judge's office, she added poison to the glass. Remember she said she found the body when she brought in fresh water for Cindi?"

"Oh! Where's that glass?"

"On Cindi's desk. Lilian switched it for the one which had held the poison and disposed of any evidence before calling us."

Patrick pulled out his phone. "Chief, we've just got to arrest the killer and we'll be right with you… Thank you, sir." He turned to Wilma. "He's putting our food over the coals right now and has a celebratory drink cooling."

They didn't need to haul the murderer over the coals as she began to confess as soon as the handcuffs went on.

Thank you for reading this book. I hope you enjoyed it. If you did, I'd really appreciate a short review on Amazon, Goodreads – or anywhere else.

To learn more about my writing life, hear about new releases and get a free exclusive ebook, sign up to my newsletter – subscribepage.io/ItLSNa or you can find the link on my website patsycollins.co.uk

<u>More Books by Patsy Collins</u>

Novels

Firestarter
Escape To The Country
A Year And A Day
Paint Me A Picture
Leave Nothing But Footprints
Acting Like A Killer

Little Mallow cosy mystery novel series

Disguised Murder and Community Spirit
in Little Mallow
Dependable Friends and Deceitful Neighbours
in Little Mallow
Deadly Words and Innocent Gossip in Little Mallow

Short story collections

Over The Garden Fence
Up The Garden Path
Through The Garden Gate
In The Garden Air
Beyond The Garden Wall

All That Love Stuff
With Love And Kisses
Lots Of Love
Love Is The Answer

No Family Secrets
Can't Choose Your Family
Keep It In The Family
Family Feeling
Happy Families

Slightly Spooky Stories I
Slightly Spooky Stories II
Slightly Spooky Stories III
Slightly Spooky Stories IV
Slightly Spooky Stories V

Just A Job
Perfect Timing
A Way With Words
Dressed To Impress
Coffee & Cake
Criminal Intent
Making A Move
Days To Remember
Not A Drop To Drink
A Clean Bill Of Health
Your Good Health

Non-fiction

From Story Idea To Reader
(co-written with Rosemary J. Kind)

A Year Of Ideas:
365 sets of writing prompts and exercises